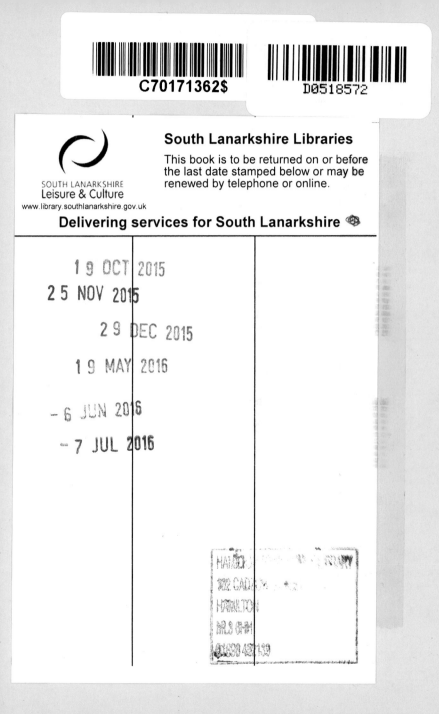

South Lanarkshire Libraries

This book is to be returned on or before the last date stamped below or may be renewed by telephone or online.

SOUTH LANARKSHIRE
Leisure & Culture
www.library.southlanarkshire.gov.uk

Delivering services for South Lanarkshire

THE SERMON ON
THE FALL OF ROME

Also by Jérôme Ferrari in English translation

Where I Left My Soul

JÉRÔME FERRARI

THE SERMON ON
THE FALL OF ROME

Translated from the French by
Geoffrey Strachan

MACLEHOSE PRESS
QUERCUS · LONDON

First published in the French language as *Le sermon sur la chute de Rome*
by Actes Sud, Arles, 2012
First published in Great Britain in 2014 by
MacLehose Press

an imprint of Quercus
55 Baker Street
7th Floor, South Block
London W1U 8EW

This book has been selected to receive financial assistance from English PEN's PEN Translates!
programme. English PEN exists to promote literature and our understanding of it,
to uphold writers' freedoms around the world, to campaign against the persecution
and imprisonment of writers for stating their views, and to promote the friendly
co-operation of writers and the free exchange of ideas.
www.englishpen.org

A CIP catalogue record for this book is available
from the British Library.

ISBN (HB) 978 0 85705 290 2
ISBN (Ebook) 978 1 78206 838 9

10 9 8 7 6 5 4 3 2

Designed and typeset in Albertina by Libanus Press, Marlborough
Printed and bound in Great Britain by Clays Ltd, St Ives plc

To my great-uncle, Antoine Vesperini

TRANSLATOR'S NOTE

Most of the action in Jérôme Ferrari's novel takes place in twentieth-century France (Corsica and Paris) and Algeria. The city of Corte was once briefly the capital of independent Corsica and is the site of the university which reopened in 1981. The "maquis", named after the low scrub that covers many hillsides in Corsica, was the term used for the resistance movement during the occupation in the Second World War. "Ribbedu", as the author notes in a footnote, was the nickname of Dominique Luccini, head of the Communist maquis in the wild Alta Rocca region of Corsica.

Several of the places in Algeria mentioned in the text, including Djemila, Tipasa and Annaba, are the sites of Roman remains. Annaba, one of the oldest cities in Algeria, was originally named Hippo. Augustine of Hippo (St Augustine) was bishop there from 396 A.D. to 430 A.D. In 430 A.D. the city fell to the Vandals. In the eighth century it was renamed Bled El-Anned (from which the modern name is derived). In 1832 the French took the city and renamed it Bône. In 1962 Algeria became independent from France.

The book contains echoes of Algeria's prehistory. The first viable state to flourish in what is now Algeria was the Berber kingdom of Numidia. In 206 B.C. the new king of eastern Numidia,

Massinissa, made an alliance with Rome to defeat the neighbouring state of Carthage. Believing himself to be betrothed to Sophonisba, the daughter of a Carthaginian general, Massinissa defeated Syphax, king of western Numidia, who was allied to Carthage. But Syphax had married Sophonisba, in his capital city of Cirta. Refusing to allow her to be taken to Rome to be displayed in a triumph, Massinissa poisoned her and then gave her a royal funeral.

I am indebted to a number of people and, in particular, the author for assistance and advice in the preparation of this translation. My thanks are due notably to Dr Thomas Anderson, Robert Caston, June Elks, Ben Faccini, Scott Grant, Willem Hackman, Wayne Holloway, Fr Nicholas King SJ, Ann Mansbridge, Richard Sorabji, Simon Strachan, Susan Strachan and Roger Watts.

G.S.

AUTHOR'S NOTE TO
THE ORIGINAL FRENCH EDITION

All the chapter titles, with the exception of the last one, are taken from Augustine's sermons. I have also quoted from the Psalms and Genesis, and have taken Shulamite's "ashen hair" (page 151) from Paul Celan's poem "Death Fugue", which was itself borrowed from the Song of Songs.

Without Daniel Istria's help I should never have been able to picture what a fifth-century African cathedral might have looked like, nor how sermons were preached there.

Jean-Alain Huser helped initiate me into the twin mysteries of French colonial administration and tropical diseases, the symptoms of which I have ventured to modify somewhat, according to criteria which I hesitate to qualify as aesthetic.

My warm thanks are due to both of them.

There are so many ways in which I am indebted to my great-uncle Antoine Vesperini that, rather than listing them all, it seemed to me simpler and more appropriate for me to dedicate this novel to him, for it could not have existed without him.

J.F.

TABLE OF CONTENTS

THE SERMON ON
THE FALL OF ROME

"Are you surprised that the end of the world is upon us? You might rather be surprised that the world has grown so old. The world is like a man; he is born, he grows up, he ages and he dies . . . In old age a man is filled with complaints and in old age the world, too, is filled with troubles . . . Christ says to you, 'The world is passing away, the world is old, the world is going under, the world is already gasping with the breathing of old age, but be not afraid, your youth shall be renewed like the eagle's.'"

SAINT AUGUSTINE

Sermon 81, paragraph 8, December 419

"If Romans are not perishing
perhaps Rome has not perished"

So, to bear witness to the beginning – as well as the end – there was this photograph, taken in the summer of 1918, which Marcel Antonetti would vainly persist in studying throughout his life, seeking to decode the enigma of the absence within it. In it his five brothers and sisters can be seen, posed there with their mother. There is a milky whiteness all around them, with no sign either of ground or walls, and they seem to be floating like ghosts amid a strange mist that will soon swallow them up and make them disappear. She sits there, dressed in mourning, unmoving and ageless, a dark scarf over her head, her hands placed flat upon her knees, staring so intensely at a spot located far beyond the lens that it is as if she were indifferent to everything around her – the photographer and his equipment, the summer sunlight and her own children, her son, Jean-Baptiste, wearing a beret with a pompom, timidly nestling up to her, squeezed into a sailor suit that is too tight for him, her three older daughters, lined up behind her, all stiff in their Sunday best, their arms rigid beside their bodies, and, on her own in the foreground, the youngest, Jeanne-Marie, barefoot and in rags, her pale, sulky little face hidden behind the long untidy locks of her black hair. And each time he meets his mother's gaze Marcel feels utterly convinced that it is directed at him, that she was already peering into limbo to seek out the eyes of the unborn son she does not yet know. For what Marcel contemplates, in this photograph taken in the course of a hot summer's day in 1918 in the school yard where an itinerant photographer had hung a white sheet between two trestles, is first and foremost his own absence. All the people are there who will soon surround him with their care, perhaps their love, but the truth is that none of them is thinking about him, and none of them miss him. They have fetched out the best clothes they never wear from a wardrobe stuffed with mothballs and have had to comfort Jeanne-Marie, who is only four and does not yet own either a new dress or shoes, before all going up to the school together, glad, no doubt, for something to be happening at last that might rescue them for a while from the monotony and solitude of all their years of war. The school yard is crowded. All through the day in the scorching heat of the summer of 1918, the photographer took pictures of women and children, of cripples, old men and priests, all filing past his camera, all of them, too, seeking some relief, and Marcel's mother, brother and sisters waited their turn patiently, from time to time drying Jeanne-Marie's tears of shame over her ragged dress and bare feet. At the moment when the picture was being taken she refused to pose with the others and had to be allowed to remain standing there all alone, in the front row, hiding beneath her tousled hair. There they all are and Marcel is not there. And yet, through the magic of a mysterious symmetry, now that he has seen them all into their graves, one after the other, they only exist thanks to him and his stubbornly faithful gaze, he, of whom, as they held their breath at the moment when the photographer released the shutter of his camera, they were not even thinking, is now their unique and fragile bulwark against nothingness, and this is why he continues to remove the photograph from the drawer where he keeps it carefully, even though he loathes it, just as, in point of fact, he has always loathed it, because if one day he neglects to do this, nothing will be left of them, the photograph will turn once more into a lifeless pattern of black and grey patches, and Jeanne-Marie will forever cease to be a little girl aged four. Sometimes he looks at them with rage, is tempted to reproach them for their lack of foresight, their ingratitude, their indifference, but he catches his mother's eye and fancies she can see him, right there in the limbo where unborn children are held captive, and is waiting for him, even if the truth is that Marcel is not, and never has been, the one her eyes are desperately searching for. For the one she is searching for, far beyond the lens, is the one who ought to be standing there beside her and whose absence is so glaring that one might think this photograph had only been taken in the summer of 1918 to make it tangible and preserve this record of it. Marcel's father was captured in the Ardennes during the early fighting and from the start of the war has been working in a salt mine in Lower Silesia. Once every two months he sends a letter which he gets one of his comrades to write and which the children study before conveying it out loud to their mother. Letters take so long to reach them that they are always afraid what they are hearing may be no more than the echo of a dead man's voice, transmitted in unfamiliar handwriting. But he is not dead and he returns to the village in February 1919, so that Marcel may see the light of day. His eyelids and lashes are burned, his fingernails are as if eaten by acid and on his cracked lips can be seen the white traces of scarred layers of skin he will never be able to shed. Doubtless he looked at his children without recognising them, but his wife had not changed, because she had never looked youthful or fresh, and he hugged her to him, although Marcel has never understood what could have drawn their two desiccated, broken bodies to one another, it could not have been desire, nor even animal instinct, perhaps it was simply because Marcel needed them to embrace in order to emerge from the limbo in whose depths he had been on the qui vive for so long, waiting to be born, and it was in response to his silent call that they had crawled on top of one another that night in the darkness of their bedroom, making no noise, so as not to alert Jean-Baptiste and Jeanne-Marie, who were pretending to be asleep, lying there with thumping hearts on their mattress in a corner of the room, witnessing the mystery of the creakings and hoarse sighs which, without finding a name for it, they understood, their minds reeling at the enormity of this mystery in which violence and intimacy were intermingled in such proximity to them, while their parents wore themselves ragged rubbing their bodies against one another, twisting and probing their own dry flesh, so as to bring back to life the ancient wellsprings made barren by sadness, mourning and salt, and draw out from the depths of their bellies what was left there of humours and mucus, albeit only a remnant of moisture, a little of the fluid that serves as the container for life, a single drop, and their efforts were so great that this unique drop did finally well up and condense within them, making life possible, even though they themselves were barely alive. Marcel has always imagined – has always feared – that he was not wanted, but simply imposed by some impenetrable cosmic necessity that allowed him to grow in his mother's arid, hostile womb just at the season when a foetid wind was arising, carrying up the miasmas of a deadly influenza from the sea and the unhealthy plains before sweeping through the villages, hurling dozens of men who had survived the war into hastily dug graves, without anything being able to halt it, like that poisonous fly of ancient legend, the fly born from the putrefaction of an accursed skull, ready to emerge one morning from the void of its empty sockets, exhaling its deadly breath and feeding upon men's lives, until it became so monstrously plump that its shadow plunged whole valleys into darkness and only the Archangel's lance could finally dispatch it. But the Archangel had long ago returned to his celestial dwelling place and remained deaf to prayers and processions, turning aside from those who were dying, the weakest being the first to go, children, old men, pregnant women, yet Marcel's mother remained upright, unshakeable and sad, and the wind blowing relentlessly all around her spared her home. It finally dropped several weeks before Marcel was born, giving way to a silence that descended on fields overgrown with brambles and weeds, on collapsed stone walls, on deserted shepherds' huts and tombs. When they prised him from his mother's womb, Marcel remained unmoving and silent for many seconds before briefly emitting a feeble cry and they had to get close to his lips to feel the warmth of a tiny breath that left no trace of condensation on mirrors. His parents had him baptised within the hour. They sat beside his cradle, gazing at him wistfully, as if they had already lost him, and that was the way they went on looking at him throughout his childhood. Each time he had a mild temperature, whenever he suffered from colic, at every coughing fit, they would watch over him like a dying child, greeting every recovery as a miracle, yet one they did not hope to see repeated, for nothing is more quickly exhausted than the uncertain mercy of God. But Marcel went on recovering and he lived, all the more stubborn for being frail, as if in the dry darkness of his mother's womb he had learned so well how to devote all his feeble resources to the exhausting task of surviving, that it had made him invulnerable. A demon prowled ceaselessly around him, and his parents dreaded its victory, but Marcel knew that it would not win, in vain did it hurl him, drained of strength, into the depths of his bed, wear him out with migraines and bouts of diarrhoea, it was not going to win, it could even creep inside him to ignite the fires of an ulcer and cause him to vomit blood so violently that Marcel had to miss a whole year of school, it was not going to win, in the end Marcel would always recover, even if he could forever feel the presence of a hand lurking in his stomach, waiting to rip into its delicate walls with sharp fingers, for such was to be the life he had been granted, always under threat and always triumphant. He was thrifty with his strength, his affection, his wonder, when Jeanne-Marie came looking for him, exclaiming, Marcel, come quickly, there's a man flying past the fountain, his heart did not start racing, nor did he bat an eyelid as he watched the first cyclist anyone had ever seen passing through the village, hurtling down the road at top speed, the sides of his jacket flapping behind him like an oystercatcher's wings and it was without emotion that he watched his father rise at dawn to go and till fields that did not belong to him and tend animals that were not his, while on all sides there arose monuments to the dead on which, with haughty and decisive gestures, women of bronze who looked like his mother each thrust out before them the child they consented to sacrifice to the *patrie*, while next to them soldiers waving flags were collapsing open-mouthed, as if it were necessary now, having already paid the price in flesh and blood, to offer a vanished world the tribute of the iconography it insisted on, before departing for ever, to make way, at last, for the new world. But nothing happened, one world had well and truly vanished but no new world arrived to take its place, and mankind, left in the lurch, lacking a world, soldiered on with the drama of procreation and death, Marcel's older sisters got married one after the other and people consumed *beignets* as they sat under a lifeless, implacable sun, drinking vile wine and forcing themselves to smile, as if something were finally about to happen, as if the women, with their children, were about to bring the new world itself into being, but nothing did happen, time brought nothing more than the monotonous succession of seasons that were all alike, promising only the curse of their inevitability. Sky, mountains and sea congealed together in the bottomless chasm of the stares of livestock, as they endlessly dragged their meagre carcases along the sides of rivers, in dust or in mud, and the staring eyes reflected by candlelight in all the mirrors in the depths of the houses, were similar, the same chasms gouged out of faces of wax. Curled up in the depths of his bed, Marcel sensed a mortal anguish clutching at his heart whenever night fell, because he knew this fathomless, silent night was not the natural and temporary continuation of the day but something terrifying, a primal state into which the earth was relapsing after twelve hours of exhausting exertion and from which it would never again break free. Dawn heralded no more than yet another temporary reprieve and Marcel would set off for school, stopping on the way from time to time to vomit blood and vowing to say nothing about it to his mother who would have made him go to bed and would have prayed, kneeling at his bedside after applying hot compresses to his stomach, and he was determined from now on not to let his demon snatch him away from the only things that gave him joy, the schoolmaster's lessons, the coloured maps and the majesty of history, the inventors and men of science, the children saved from rabies, the princes and kings, everything that enabled him to believe that there was a world beyond the sea, a world throbbing with life, in which men still knew how to do something other than drag out their existence in suffering and disarray, a world that could inspire other desires than that of leaving it as quickly as possible, for he was sure that beyond the sea they would already, for years now, have been celebrating the arrival of a new world, the one Jean-Baptiste had gone off to join in 1926, lying about his age so that he could enlist, obliterate the sea and finally discover what a world might be like, in the company of those young men fleeing with him in their hundreds, whose resigned parents, despite the wrench of parting, could find no arguments to hold them back. At table, sitting next to Jeanne-Marie, Marcel ate with his eyes shut, so as to voyage with Jean-Baptiste on fabulous oceans alive with piratical junks, visit pagan cities that teemed with chanting, smoke and cries, and walk in perfumed jungles, peopled by wild animals and fearsome natives, who would view his brother with respect and terror, as if he were the invincible Archangel, the destroyer of scourges, once again devoted to men's salvation, and during the catechism he would listen with sealed lips to the lies told by the evangelist, for he knew what an apocalypse was, he knew that at the end of the world the heavens did not open and there were neither horsemen nor trumpets nor number of the beast, no monster, but only silence, so much so that you might think nothing had happened. And indeed, nothing had happened, the years trickled away like sand, and still nothing happened and this nothing spread the power of its blind reign over everything, a deadly and fruitless reign, so that no-one could any longer say when it had begun. For at the moment during the summer of 1918 when that photograph was taken, to ensure that something might be left to bear witness to the beginning and also the end, the world had already vanished, it had vanished without anyone noticing and it was, above all, its absence, the most enigmatic and the most daunting of all those absences captured that day on paper by the silver salts, that Marcel would spend his life contemplating, searching for traces of it in the milky whiteness with its faded edges, in the faces of his mother, his brother and his sisters, in Jeanne-Marie's sulky pout, in the insignificance of their wretched human presences, as the ground gave way beneath their feet, giving them no choice but to float aimlessly like ghosts in an abstract and infinite space from which there was no escape, one from which even the love that bound them together could not save them, because in the absence of a world, love itself is powerless. It is true

28

that we do not know what worlds are, nor what their existence depends on. Perhaps somewhere in the universe the mysterious law is written that presides over their origins, their growth and their ending. But this we do know: for a new world to arise, first an old world must die. And we also know that the interval that separates them can be infinitely brief or, on the other hand, so long that men have to spend dozens of years learning to live amid the desolation before discovering, inevitably, that they are incapable of doing so and that, in the final reckoning, they have not lived. Perhaps we can even identify the almost imperceptible signs that proclaim the recent disappearance of a world, not screaming shells above the gutted plains of the North, but the release of a shutter, scarcely disturbing the vibrant summer light, or the delicate, damaged hand of a young woman very gently closing a door in the middle of the night on what should not have been her life, or the square sail of a ship crossing the blue waters of the Mediterranean, in the open sea off Hippo, bringing the inconceivable news from Rome that men still exist but their world is no more.

"Then do not feel reluctance, my brothers,
towards the chastisements of God"

In the middle of the night, taking good care to make no noise, although there was nobody to hear her, Hayet closed the door of the little flat she had lived in for eight years above the bar where she worked as a barmaid, and disappeared. Around ten o'clock in the morning the hunters came back from the drive. The hounds on the trucks' loading bays by the bar, still excited by the chase and the scent of blood, were jostling one another, frantically wagging their tails, moaning and barking hysterically, which the men, almost as happy and over-excited as they were, responded to with oaths and curses, and Virgile Ordioni's vast frame was convulsed with suppressed laughter, while the others clapped him on the shoulder in congratulation, because he had single-handedly killed three of the five boars of the morning, and Virgile was blushing and laughing, while Vincent Leandri, who had pathetically missed a big male less than thirty yards off, was lamenting the fact that he was no longer good for anything and remarking that the only reason he persisted in coming on the drives was for the apéritif afterwards, and then someone called out that the bar was closed. Hayet had always been as regular and reliable as the stars in their courses and Vincent at once imagined that some mishap had befallen her. He ran up to the flat, knocked at the door, softly at first, and then hammering away, but still to no avail, and called out,

"Hayet, Hayet, are you alright? Answer me, please,"
and then announced that he was going to break the door down. Someone suggested to Vincent that he should calm down, Hayet could have gone out on an urgent errand even though it was very hard, virtually impossible, in fact, to imagine any kind of errand one might have in the village in early autumn especially on a Sunday morning and moreover an errand so urgent that it warranted closing the bar, but then you never knew, and Hayet would certainly be back, but she did not come back and Vincent kept saying that now he really was going to knock the door down, and it was becoming increasingly difficult to restrain him and in the end everyone agreed that the logical solution would be to go and inform Marie-Angèle Susini that, improbable as it might seem, her barmaid was missing. Marie-Angèle received them with incredulity and even suspected them of already being drunk and playing a cruel trick on her, but apart from Virgile, who was still laughing from time to time without knowing why, they all seemed worn out and weary, perfectly sober and vaguely uneasy and Vincent Leandri even seemed distraught, so much so that Marie-Angèle picked up the duplicate keys to the bar and the flat and went with them, herself increasingly uneasy, and hurried

upstairs to open Hayet's flat. It had been meticulously cleaned, there was no speck of dust, the crockery and taps were gleaming, the cupboards and drawers were empty, the sheets and pillow-cases on the bed had been changed, nothing was left of Hayet, not so much as an earring fallen behind a piece of furniture, nor a stray hair grip in a corner of the bathroom, not a scrap of paper, not even a hair, and Marie-Angèle was surprised to detect no scent other than that of cleaning products, as if no human being had lived there for years. Looking round at the dead flat, she could not understand why Hayet had left like that, without a parting word, but she knew that she would never return and she would never see her again. She heard a voice saying,

"We really ought to call the law,"
but she shook her head sadly and no-one insisted, because it was evident that the silent tragedy that had been played out here, at an unknown time in the night, concerned only one person, adrift in the depths of a lonely heart, to which human society could no longer render justice. They all went quiet for a while, then one of them ventured timidly,

"Seeing as you're here, Marie-Angèle, the bar, you know, you could open it, and then we could have our apéritif after all,"
and Marie-Angèle nodded silently. A murmur of satisfaction ran through the group of huntsmen, Virgile began laughing very loudly and they moved towards the bar with the hounds baying and groaning in the sunlight and Vincent Leandri muttered,

"What a right bunch of drunken bastards you are,"
before following them into the bar. Behind the counter Marie-Angèle once more went back to the routines that she knew so well and would have so much liked to have forgotten, busying herself deftly amid the glasses and ice buckets, mentally noting the orders for rounds of drinks belted out at an infernal pace by thunderous voices of increasing unsteadiness, registering each one as it came and without the slightest error, listening to the disjointed conversations, the same tales told a hundred times before with variations and improbable exaggerations, about how Virgile Ordioni always made a point of slicing fine strips of liver from the dead boar's smoking entrails, and consuming them on the spot, all warm and raw, with the composure of a prehistoric man, despite the cries of disgust to which he would respond by invoking the memory of his poor father who had always taught him there was nothing better for the health, and now the same exclamations of disgust rang round the bar, with clenched fists pounding on the zinc-topped counter, all spattered with pastis, and there was more laughter and it was observed that Virgile was an animal but a bloody good shot, and, all alone in a corner, Vincent Leandri stared at his glass, his eyes full of despair. The more time passed, the clearer it became to Marie-Angèle that she was not prepared to take up this work again, for it had become even more intolerable to her than she would have expected. For years she had relied on Hayet, gradually leaving all the management of the bar to her, in total confidence,

as if she had been part of the family and Marie-Angèle felt cut to the quick to think that she could have left without even coming to kiss her goodbye or leaving a farewell message, just a few lines to prove to her that something had happened here, something that had mattered, but this, Marie-Angèle perceived, was precisely what Hayet could not do, for it was evident that she had wanted not only to vanish but also to wipe away all the years spent here, retaining from them only her beautiful hands, prematurely ruined, which she might have wanted to cut off and leave behind her if that had been possible, and the furiously obsessive way she had cleaned the flat was simply the evidence of a fierce desire for erasure and of a belief that by an act of will one could obliterate from one's own life all the years one wished one had never lived through, even if this meant erasing the very memory of those who have loved us. And as she poured yet another round of pastis into glasses so full that there was no longer any room for water in them, Marie-Angèle found herself hoping that Hayet, wherever she was and whatever destination she was headed for, might be feeling, if not happy, at least liberated and Marie-Angèle summoned up all the resources of her love to bless her and to let her departure be marred by no resentment. Thus it was that Hayet went on her way, untouched by blessings and resentment alike, not suspecting that her disappearance had already caused an upheaval in a world that was itself no longer in her thoughts, for Marie-Angèle now knew for certain she was never going to open up the bar again, she was never again going to inflict on herself the spectacle of the filthy yellowish soup crystallising in dirty glasses, the smell of aniseed-flavoured breath, and the shouts of the card players at their belote in the depths of interminable winters, the recollection of which filled her with nausea, as did that of the incessant arguments with their ritual but empty threats inevitably followed by tearful and, of course, undying, reconciliations. She knew she could not do it. Her daughter, Virginie, would have had to run the bar in her place until she could recruit a new barmaid, but this solution was impossible to contemplate from every point of view. Virginie had never done anything in her life remotely resembling work, she had always been a pioneer in the infinite fields of lethargy and listlessness, and seemed firmly resolved to pursue this vocation to the end, but even if she had been a workaholic her glum temperament and regal airs made her quite unsuited to the performance of a task that involved having regular contact with other human beings, albeit those as uncouth as the bar's regular customers. Of course Marie-Angèle would be able to find another barmaid in the end, but she felt herself to be incapable of stepping into the role of *patronne* once more, she bridled at supervising the opening hours and doing the till every evening to check that the accounts were correct, she had no more appetite for acting out the whole performance of authority and vigilance which Hayet had for so long rendered totally superfluous and, in particular, she was loath to admit that Hayet might well, all things considered, be replaceable. She watched Virgile Ordioni staggering towards the toilets, and brooded stoically on the sad fate that awaited the impeccably disinfected lavatory seat, not to mention the floor and walls, picturing herself spending the whole of Sunday afternoon, sponge in hand, cursing these savages, and decided to advertise for someone to manage the bar.

That evening, having first given her son, Libero, detailed news of each of his brothers and sisters, and then of the numberless cohort of his nephews and nieces and after asking him, as she had done every night since he got there, if he was settling down alright in Paris, Gavina Pintus told him, just before hanging up, that the barmaid at the bar had mysteriously left the village. Libero passed this on to Matthieu Antonetti, who responded with an absent-minded grunt, and they turned back to their work, instantly forgetting something that had nevertheless just marked the start of what would be a new existence for them. They had known one another since childhood, though not for the whole of their lives. Matthieu was eight when his mother, concerned about his resolutely solitary and contemplative character, decided that he needed a friend to enjoy his summer holidays in the village. So she took him by the hand, having sprinkled him with eau de cologne, and led him along to see the Pintus family, whose youngest son was the same age as him. Their vast house was ornamented with various excrescences made of breeze blocks which they had left unplastered and it looked like an organism that had never stopped growing in erratic fashion, as if driven by some vital and primeval force, electric cables decorated with dangling light sockets ran along the facades, the courtyard was piled high with chimney pots, wheelbarrows, tiles, dogs asleep in the sun, bags of cement and a considerable number of unidentified objects biding their time in the expectation of finally proving their usefulness one day. Gavina Pintus was mending a jacket, and her body, rendered shapeless by eleven pregnancies that had fulfilled their term, spilled out of a frail deck-chair, Libero sat on a wall behind her, watching three of his brothers totally smeared in grease busying themselves around a venerable motor car whose engine had been stripped down. When he saw Matthieu approaching, resisting the vigorous tugging of his mother by making himself increasingly heavy at the end of her arm, Libero stared at him attentively, unmoving and unsmiling, and Matthieu made himself so heavy that Claudie Antonetti was compelled to come to a halt, and after several seconds, he dissolved into tears so utterly that she had no option but to take him home to blow his nose and lecture him. He ended up taking refuge in the arms of his big sister, Aurélie, who once again performed her role as proxy mother with a wholly childish gravity. At the end of the afternoon Libero came and knocked at their door and Matthieu agreed to go with him into the village and allow himself to be led into a jumble of secret pathways, springs, fantastical insects and alleyways that little by little fitted together into a coherent space and formed a world that rapidly ceased to terrify him and became his obsession. The more the years passed the more the end of the summer holidays gave rise to painful scenes, to an extent that Claudie sometimes regretted having thrust her son along the road to a social integration whose consequences she had not foreseen. Matthieu now lived only for the start of the summer and when in his thirteenth year he grasped that his parents, like utterly selfish monsters, were not for a moment planning to abandon their work in Paris so as to allow him to settle permanently in the village, he badgered them to at least send him there during the Christmas holidays. Matthieu's response to their refusal was a quite disgraceful series of hysterical fits and bouts of fasting too brief to damage his health but sufficiently long and dramatic to exasperate his parents. Gloomily Jacques and Claudie Antonetti observed to one another that they had bred an appalling little brat, but this depressing observation was no help at all in resolving their problem. Jacques and Claudie were first cousins. After his wife had died in childbirth, Marcel Antonetti, Jacques's father, had proclaimed that he was incapable of looking after an infant and had turned for help, as he had done all his life, to his sister, Jeanne-Marie, who, without pausing for thought, had immediately taken Jacques in, to bring him up with her daughter, Claudie. Thus they had grown up together and the discovery that they were lovers, soon followed by the public announcement of their intention to marry was, not surprisingly, greeted with stunned indignation by the entire family. But so stubborn were they that in the end the marriage took place, in the presence of a meagre gathering, for whom this ceremony in no way represented the touching triumph of love but rather that of vice and incest. The birth of Aurélie, who was, against all expectation, a perfectly healthy baby, went some way to pacify family tensions and Matthieu's arrival took place in an apparent atmosphere of perfect normality. But it quickly became apparent that Marcel, being incapable of venting his spleen on his son or his daughter-in-law, had transferred his hostility onto his grandchildren, and although he finally, in spite of himself, came to be fond of Aurélie, to the point of occasionally indulging in displays of senile adulation, he continued to persecute Matthieu with malevolence, even hatred, however incongruous such a sentiment may seem, as if the little boy had himself arranged the abominable union from which he had sprung. Every summer Claudie would intercept the hostile looks he darted at her son, each time Matthieu went up to him to kiss him he made gestures of recoil too obvious for them to have been instinctive, and he never missed an opportunity to make cutting observations to him about the way he sat at table or his propensity for dirtiness or stupidity, and Jacques would lower his eyes in a pained manner while Claudie restrained herself twenty times a day from abusing this old man for whom she no longer had the least affection. When Matthieu began spending time with Libero, Marcel's conduct had been a disgrace, through clenched teeth he would mutter,

"So now he's besotted with a Sardinian, well, that doesn't surprise me,"

and Claudie held her tongue,

"But you'd think he could refrain from bringing him back here to the house,"

and she had held her tongue, for years she had held her tongue. But a few weeks later Matthieu had sent a card to his grandfather for his birthday.

"Happy birthday, with love from your grandson, Matthieu," a harmless, ritual card, to which Marcel had sent a two-line reply:

"My boy, at the age of nearly thirteen, please spare me your idiotic nonsense. It is inappropriate to my age and no longer appropriate to yours. If you have something to tell me, write. Otherwise, desist."

Claudie had intercepted this letter and picked up the telephone shaking with fury.

"You're a stupid old bastard, Uncle Marcel, and no doubt you'll die a stupid old bastard, but meanwhile I advise you never to write like that to my son again,"

and Marcel had begun vaguely whimpering down the phone until Claudie hung up on him, cursing the cruel injustice of a fate that had seen fit to deprive her of her own parents while taking good care to spare this intolerable old fart, who was forever complaining that he was at death's door and rang up in the middle of the night over the slightest cold or the most minor ailment, waxing endlessly eloquent about the cunning progress of the ulcer that should have killed him seventy years ago, whereas in fact he had an iron constitution, as if, having totally neglected his son as a child, he were particularly determined to ruin his life in adulthood, and Claudie dreamed of a delicious plan whereby she would catch the plane out there and go to the village to suffocate him with a cushion or, better still, throttle him with her bare hands, but she was forced to abandon her revenge fantasies, while noting that in the real world she could not possibly entrust her son to this man during the Christmas holidays, nor could she possibly tell him that he must stay in Paris because his paternal grandfather hated him. It was a telephone call to Gavina Pintus that resolved the problem: in a mixture of Corsican and her Barbaggia region Sardinian she declared that she would be delighted for Matthieu to stay with her any time he wanted. Claudie was tempted to refuse, if only to teach Matthieu that emotional blackmail never paid, all the more because she suspected him of being, via Libero, the originator of this most opportune invitation, but she soon accepted it when she realised that it was now she who was in a position to blackmail her son, and she never hesitated to do so, invoking the threat of a cancelled holiday at every lapse on the school front or attempt at rebellion, and over the years she rejoiced to note that, in truth, as the daily spectacle of a courteous, industrious and obedient son confirmed, nothing paid so well as blackmail.

There were two worlds, there may have been an infinite number of others but for him there were just two. Two completely separate worlds, each with its own hierarchy, without shared frontiers, and the one he wanted to make his own was the one that was the most foreign to him. It was as if he had discovered that the essential part of himself was precisely the one that was the most foreign and he now needed to explore it and be reunited with it, because it had been torn away from him long before his birth and he had been condemned to live the life of a foreigner, without his even being aware of it, the life in which everything was familiar to him had become hateful, it was no life at all, it was a mechanical parody of the life he now wanted to forget, for example, by feeling the cold wind from the mountain lashing his face as he and Libero rode along on the back of a jolting 4x4 driven by Sauveur Pintus up the rutted road that led to his mountain hut. Matthieu was sixteen and now spent all his winter holidays at the village and moved around amid the intricacies of the Pintus tribe with the ease of a seasoned ethnologist. Libero's older brother had invited them to come and spend the day with him and when they got there they found Virgile Ordioni busy castrating some young boars gathered together in a pen. He lured them with food while emitting variously modulated grunts which were considered attractive to porcine ears, and when one of them, spellbound by the charm of this music or, more prosaically, blinded by greed, incautiously came close, Virgile jumped on it, flung it to the ground like a sack of potatoes, caught it by the hind legs and turned it over before straddling its belly, the implacable vice of his massive thighs gripping the misguided animal, which now uttered appalling squeals, doubtless sensing that nothing good was coming its way and Virgile, knife in hand, sliced into the scrotum with a practised action and plunged his fingers into the opening to extract a first testicle, and cut the cord, before dealing with the second in the same way and tossing them together into a large bowl that was half full. As soon as the operation was completed the liberated porker, displaying a stoicism that Matthieu found impressive, began feeding again, just as if nothing had happened, there among its heedless fellows, which all, one after the other, passed through Virgile's expert hands. Matthieu and Libero watched the spectacle leaning on a fence. Sauveur emerged from the farm and came to join them.

"You've never seen the like of that before, have you, Matthieu?"

Matthieu shook his head and Sauveur gave a little laugh.

"He's good, Virgile. He knows how it's done. There's no more to be said."

But Matthieu was not thinking of saying anything at all, not least because the pen was now an arena for an interesting turn of events. Virgile, seated on a pig whose scrotum he had just cut open, let fly an oath and turned to Sauveur, who asked him what was up.

"There's only one here. Just the one! The other one hasn't come down!"

Sauveur shrugged his shoulders.

"That happens."

But Virgile was not prepared to admit defeat. He cut off the single testicle and continued rummaging in the empty scrotum, shouting,

"I can feel it! I can feel it!"

and went on cursing because the pig, that was paying very dearly for its late puberty, was making desperate efforts to escape its tormentor's grip, it twisted this way and that, the dust flew, and it uttered cries that now seemed almost human, so that Virgile eventually gave up. The pig stood up and sought refuge in a corner of the pen, with a sullen air and shaking legs, its long ears, spotted with black, dangling over its eyes.

"Will it die?" asked Matthieu.

Virgile joined them, the bowl under his arm, wiping the sweat from his brow and laughed and said,

"Oh no, he'll not die. He's just a bit dazed. They're tough, pigs. They don't die like that,"

and he laughed again and asked,

"Well, lads, how's it going? Shall we go and eat?"

and Matthieu realised that the bowl contained their meal and tried not to let any of his surprise show because this was his world, even if all of it was not yet known to him, and each surprise, however daunting, must be denied on the spot and made over into habit, though in this case the dullness of habit was a far cry from the relish Matthieu felt as he stuffed himself with pigs' balls grilled over a wood fire, while a great wind drove the clouds towards the mountain, above a little chapel dedicated to the Virgin, a completely white chapel at whose foot burned the scarlet candles Sauveur and Virgile occasionally lit in honour of their companion in solitude, and the hands that had built this chapel had long since been swept away by the wind, but they had left traces of their existence here, and higher up, along a steep slope, the remains of collapsed walls could be seen, almost invisible because they were of the same red colour as the granite rock from whence they had arisen before the mountain took them back, slowly absorbing them into its bosom, all covered in stones and thistles, as if to make a show, not of its power, but of its tenderness. Sauveur heated a pan of terrible coffee on the fire, speaking to Virgile and his brother in a language Matthieu did not understand but knew to be his own, and he listened to them, as he drank the boiling hot coffee, fancying that he could understand them, although their words had no more meaning for him than the roar of the river whose unseen torrents could be heard surging along the base of a steep chasm that ripped through the mountain like a deep wound, a furrow traced by God's finger at the beginning of the world. After the meal they followed Virgile into a room where cheeses were drying and he opened a vast old trunk that was filled with an appalling collection of relics, curb bits, rusty old stirrups, pairs of military boots of all sizes with leather so stiff they seemed as if made of bronze, and he took out an army rifle wrapped in rags, as well as various pieces of ironmongery which Matthieu was amazed to learn were Sten guns that had been parachuted down in such great numbers that they could still be found in the maquis, where they had been waiting for sixty years to be retrieved, and Virgile laughed and told them his father had been a great resistance fighter, the terror of the Italians, in the days when Ribeddu and his men trod the same ground, moving silently at night, their ears cocked for the sound of aircraft engines, and Virgile patted Matthieu on the shoulder as he listened open-mouthed, picturing himself as a formidable hero, too.

"Come on. We're going to fire it."

Virgile checked the rifle, took some bullets and they went and sat on a great rock overhanging the ravine and, one after the other, they fired across at the mountain's opposing face, the echo of the shots was lost in the forest of Vaddi Mali and great drifts of mist were now rising up from the sea and the valley, Matthieu felt cold, the recoil from the rifle hurt his shoulder and his happiness was complete.

Contrary to all expectations, Hayet's departure marked the start of a series of disasters that fell upon the village bar like the plagues of Egypt. Yet everything had seemed so promising: hardly had Marie-Angèle Susini announced that a vacancy for a manager had come up than a candidate made himself known. He was a man of about thirty who came from a little town on the coast where he had for a long time worked as waiter and barman at establishments he confidently characterised as prestigious. He was literally brimming over with enthusiasm, without doubt the bar had remarkable commercial potential, which would soon be revealed, just so long as an able manager knew how to exploit it, which, with all due respect to Marie-Angèle, had not hitherto been the case, of course, not everyone chose to be ambitious, but he, for one, was, and vastly so, and wouldn't be content to run a sleepy little establishment, the clientele from the village would not suffice for him, you couldn't do business worthy of the name with card players and the local boozers, you needed to target youth and tourists, market a concept, buy a sound system, serve light meals, he also envisaged installing a kitchen, bringing in D.J.s from the mainland, he knew the night scene like the back of his hand and he paced up and down in the bar, pointing out everything that would definitely have to be changed, starting with the furnishings that were enough to make you weep, and, when Marie-Angèle told him that, based on the turnover, she was asking twelve thousand euros as a fee for the management agreement plus the rent, he raised his arms to heaven and exclaimed that it was a bargain, Marie-Angèle would soon be amazed by the transformation she witnessed and for which he would be the project manager, twelve thousand euros was nothing, a gift, he was embarrassed by it, he felt as if he were robbing her and he explained that he planned to invest his capital in the initially necessary works and would pay her the first half of the fee within six months and the balance six months later, plus a year in advance. Marie-Angèle judged the offer a fair one and refused to listen to reason when Vincent Leandri came and warned her that, according to his enquiries, the fellow was a notorious layabout whose only professional experience amounted to a few seasonal jobs at seaside chip stalls. However, it seemed as if Vincent had proved to be unjustly suspicious. The agreed works were undertaken. The back room was transformed into a kitchen, the furnishings changed, hi-fi material, a sound system, record decks and a magnificent French bar-billiard table were delivered, and, on the eve of the opening, an illuminated sign was hung up above the door. It showed the winking face of Che Guevara, from which a cartoon strip bubble emerged, announcing in neon blue letters,

El Commandante Bar, sound, food, lounge.

The following day, at the inaugural evening, the regulars from the village were greeted by the sound of heavy techno that made it impossible for them to hear themselves yelling during their game of belote and discovered to their amazement that, for prestige reasons, the manager had decided not to serve pastis and was offering ruinously expensive cocktails instead, which they drank pulling faces, and that furthermore there was no way for them to get served again because the manager was busy making merry with a gang of his friends who were downing vast quantities of vodka and ended up dancing naked to the waist on the counter. The friends in question very rapidly became the only regular customers for the bar and the opening hours were reduced to a strict minimum. In the morning it remained closed. At around six in the evening the pounding rhythm of the techno announced the serving of apéritifs. Unfamiliar cars would park all over the place, laughter and shouts could be heard until about eleven in the evening, at which time the whole gang, including the manager, would go down into the town. Around four o'clock in the morning, on their return from a nightclub, the music would start up again, and through their shutters the villagers, doomed to insomnia, would see the manager, with an entourage of appalling-looking girls, crowding into the bar, the door of which was then locked, and rumour had it that the French bar-billiard table had only been bought so as to afford the new manager the level

53

surface he needed for the satisfaction of his lewd desires. At the end of three months Marie-Angèle went to see him and asked him how he was planning to pay the sum owing. He told her not to worry, but she thought it prudent to go again accompanied by Vincent Leandri, who demanded to see the accounts and warned him that if his legitimate curiosity were not satisfied he would be compelled to resort to extreme measures. The manager tried to prevaricate before finally admitting that there was no account book, every evening he took the entire contents of the till and spent them in the town, but that he was confident he could make good in the spring once the first tourists arrived. Vincent sighed.

"You're going to pay what you owe next week or I'll break all your teeth."

The manager's fatalistic response was not lacking in a certain nobility.

"I haven't got a bean. Nothing. I'm afraid you're going to have to break my teeth."

Marie-Angèle restrained Vincent and tried to reach some accommodation, but this proved to be impossible, for not only was there not a single sou for the fee but the suppliers had not been paid and the building works had all been done on credit. Vincent clenched his fists as Marie-Angèle tugged him outside, repeating there's no point, there's no point, but he made an about turn, took hold of a carafe and broke it over the manager's head. The latter collapsed with a groan, Vincent was panting with rage.

"It's a matter of principle, for fuck's sake, a matter of principle!"

So Marie-Angèle had to forgo her payment and settle debts she had not even incurred. She resolved to be more circumspect in choosing next time, but this did not do her much good. The management was now entrusted to a charming young couple whose conjugal strife transformed the bar into a no man's land from which, by day as well as by night, there arose a din of broken glass, shouting and oaths of unbelievable coarseness, followed by breathless reconciliations, equally unsparing in decibels, whence it emerged that, when it came to coarseness, the couple had unlimited resources, both in rage and in ecstasy, such that scandalised mothers forbade their innocent offspring to go anywhere near this place of debauchery until the young couple were replaced by a lady of perfectly respectable age and appearance who spent her days ranting at the customers and subjecting the prices of drinks to whimsical variations, as if she were devoting every ounce of her energy to ruining her own business, which she achieved in record time and, as she saw summer approaching, Marie-Angèle was in despair, convinced that she was going to have to take matters in hand herself and make good the damage done before it became irreversible. But in June, when she was almost resigned to having to go back to work herself, she received an offer which overwhelmed her with joy. They came from the mainland. For fifteen years they had been running a bar as a family business in the suburbs of Strasbourg and were now in search of a sunnier clime. Bernard Gratas and his wife had three rather ugly but well-behaved children aged between twelve and eighteen, and came with a bedridden grandmother, who had dementia, and whose senility greatly reassured Marie-Angèle. She needed stability and the Gratas family were stability incarnate. When she explained to them that, having suffered painful inconveniences on the subject of which she had no wish to elaborate, she preferred to be paid in advance, Bernard Gratas made out a cheque to her on the spot, which miraculously proved to be funded, and Marie-Angèle handed over the keys for the bar and the flat to them, restraining herself as she did so from flinging her arms about them. The grandmother was settled in beside the fireplace and the Gratas family reopened the bar, now appropriately renamed the Bar des Chasseurs, which, while it lacked originality, was redolent of the best type of traditionalism, and the bruised regulars resumed their old habits, coffee in the morning, games of cards at the apéritif hour and animated debates during the sweet summer nights. Marie-Angèle was delighted, while blaming herself for not having realised long before what her mistake had been. She should not at any price have entrusted her bar to compatriots, if she had given it a moment's thought, she would at once have looked for a manager from the mainland, the success of the Gratas couple confirmed this to her in a striking manner, simple, hard-working people, whose firm grasp of reality compensated substantially for their manifest lack of imagination, that was what she had needed all along and she had no doubt that they would end up fitting in completely, even if for the moment the villagers, with their somewhat rough-hewn concept of hospitality, never referred to them as anything other than "the Gauls" and only spoke to them to order drinks, everything would turn out for the best, and, as it happened, the more the summer continued, the more the atmosphere became, if not friendly, at least relaxed, and Bernard Gratas was now invited to join games of belote, and Vincent Leandri even decided to shake him by the hand, and soon other customers at the bar followed suit, and only a little more time was needed for the lasting harmony Marie-Angèle dreamed of to settle in. She paid no attention to some signs that should have made her uneasy. Gratas was no longer content simply to serve rounds of drinks, more and more often he would accept a drink himself, to give pleasure to all concerned, and he also began leaving first two, and soon three, buttons of his shirt undone, now favouring a tight-fitting cut, a gold bracelet mysteriously made its appearance about his wrist and, to crown it all, towards the end of the summer he made two acquisitions, a jacket of aged leather and a pair of beard clippers, which, to an alerted eye, of course, could presage only the worst.

Early in July when Matthieu and Libero arrived in the village from Paris with their degrees under their belts, Bernard Gratas had not yet embarked on the outward transformation that would soon be symptomatic of a more substantial and irreversible inner turmoil. Standing there behind the counter, sober and upright, a cloth in his hand, close beside his wife, who watched over the till, he appeared immune to any conceivable form of turmoil, something Libero summed up in a single concise observation:

"Well, he looks like a total arsehole."

But neither he nor Matthieu had plans to embark on any bond of friendship with Gratas and were too happy to be on holiday to take any more interest in the matter. They began going out every evening. They met girls. They took them for midnight bathes and sometimes brought them up to the village. They went down again with them at dawn and combined this with drinking coffee at the harbour. The cruise liners unloaded their monstrous cargoes of human flesh. Everywhere there were people, shorts, flip-flops, and cries of wonder to be heard, as well as inane remarks.

Everywhere there was life, too much life. And they watched this swarming life with an unutterable sense of superiority and relief, as if it were not of the same species as their own, because they were at home on the island, even if they, too, had to go back in September. Matthieu had never known anything else apart from these perpetual comings and goings but it was the first time Libero had returned after such a long absence. His parents had migrated there from the Barbaggia district of Sardinia in the 1960s like so many others, but he himself had never set foot there. He only knew it from his mother's recollections, a wretched land, old women with veils carefully knotted below their lower lips, men with leather gaiters, whose limbs, ribcages and skulls had been measured by generations of Italian criminologists, carefully noting the imperfections in the bone structure so as to decode its secret language and identify within it the undoubted traces of a natural propensity for crime and savagery. A vanished land. A land that no longer concerned him. Libero was the youngest of eleven brothers and sisters, of whom Sauveur, the eldest, was nearly twenty-five years his senior. Libero had never known the hatred and insults that awaited the Sardinian immigrants here, the poorly paid work, the contempt, the half-drunk driver of the school bus who used to hit children when they passed by close to him, remarking,

"There's nothing but Sardinians and Arabs in this country these days!"

and who would dart murderous looks at them in his rear-view mirror.

Times change, the terrorised children who used to lie low at the back of the bus, their heads huddled into their shoulders, had grown into men and the driver had died without anyone thinking of paying his grave the tribute of spitting on it. Libero felt at home. He had not only a complete but a quite brilliant school career behind him and after his *baccalauréat* all his applications for admission to a senior preparatory class at university had been accepted and his mother had almost suffocated with happiness, even though she had not the least idea what a senior preparatory class was, as well as suffocating Libero for good measure by hugging him to her enormous bosom, now swollen with emotion and pride. Libero had chosen to go to Bastia and for two years every Monday morning one or other of his brothers and sisters would get up in the middle of the night to drive him to Porto-Vecchio where he caught the bus. In Paris Matthieu had asked his parents to let him join the course at Bastia as well. They would have agreed but his exam results were not such that he could contemplate this, as he himself had to concede. So he enrolled at Paris IV University to read philosophy, the only subject in which he had done reasonably well, and resigned himself to travelling by métro every morning to the hideous complex at the Porte de Clignancourt. His conviction that he was a temporary recluse in a foreign world that only existed in parenthesis did not help him to make friends. He felt as if he were rubbing shoulders with ghosts with whom he had nothing in common and whom, what is more, he considered to be insufferably arrogant, as if the fact of studying philosophy conferred on them the privilege of understanding the meaning of a world in which the ordinary run of mortals were simply content to survive. Despite this, he formed a bond with one of his fellow students, Judith Haller, with whom he worked from time to time, and with whom he went to the cinema occasionally, or to have a drink in the evening. She was extremely intelligent and ebullient and the fact that she was not particularly good looking would not have been enough to put Matthieu off, but he found it impossible, at least here in Paris, to fall in love with anyone at all, because he was not destined to remain there and did not want to lie to anyone. And thus it was that, in the name of a future as insubstantial as mist, he deprived himself of the present, as so often happens with men, if the truth be told. One evening they were drinking and talking until late in a bar on the Place de la Bastille and Matthieu let the time for the last métro slip by. Judith offered to put him up and he walked home with her, after sending a text to his mother. Judith lived in a wretched *chambre de bonne* on the sixth floor of a block of flats in the twelfth arrondissement. She left the light off, put on some soft music and lay down on the bed, in T-shirt and pants, facing the window. When Matthieu lay down beside her, fully dressed, she turned to him without saying a word, he could see her eyes shining in the darkness, it seemed to him as if she were smiling a trembling smile and he could hear her deep, heavy breathing and was moved by it, he knew that all he needed to do was to reach out his hand and caress her for something to happen, but he could not, it was as if he had already abandoned and betrayed her, he was paralysed with guilt and did not stir, simply facing her and looking into her eyes until her smile vanished and they both fell asleep. He cared for her as he would for a future possibility in his life. Sometimes, when they were drinking coffee together, he imagined lifting his hand to stroke her cheek, he could sometimes almost picture this notional hand travelling up unhurriedly through the transparent air and brushing against a lock of Judith's hair before alighting on her face, whose warmth he felt in the hollow of his palm, as she gently let it happen, suddenly so solemn and silent, and he was aware, so strongly that his real heart began thumping, that he was not going to leap across the abyss that lay between him and this possible world, because, in attaining it, he would also destroy it. It was a world that could only endure in this fashion, halfway between being and nothingness, and Matthieu carefully held it there, in a complex mesh of unfulfilled acts, desire, revulsion and flesh not to be touched, without knowing that, years later, the collapse of the world he was soon going to choose to bring into existence would restore him to Judith, as to a lost home, and that he would then reproach himself for having been so cruelly mistaken about where his destiny lay. But for the moment Judith was not his destiny and he did not want her to become it, she remained simply an inoffensive and gentle pretext for dreaming, thanks to whom the barely perceptible passage of time that so stifled him, dragging him along so slowly, occasionally became swifter and lighter, and when two years had passed and the question came up of where Libero would now enrol for his studies, Matthieu was grateful to Judith, as if she had enabled him to escape from the viscous clutches of a time that never ended, which, but for her, would have held him captive. Matthieu hoped that Libero would come to Paris to continue his studies, he had such high hopes of this that he did not for a moment imagine things turning out differently, given that reality must inevitably, at least from time to time, correspond to what he hoped for. So he was seriously put out to learn that Libero was going to study literature at Corte, not from choice, but because the Pintus family did not have the means to send him to the mainland. Matthieu now had no further doubt that a malign and perverse divinity governed events here on earth in a way that was transforming his life into a long series of misfortunes and undeserved disappointments and he would doubtless have gone on believing this for a long time if an initiative of his mother's had not led him to question this disturbing hypothesis. Claudie had come to sit beside him as he brooded there gloomily, in the middle of the living room, so that nobody should escape the spectacle of his misery, studying him with an amused compassion he had been on the brink of taking offence at.

But he did not have time. First she smiled at him.

"We're going to invite Libero to come and stay here with us. In Aurélie's room. What do you think about that?"

That summer, just as he had done at the age of eight, he went with her to see the Pintus family. Gavina Pintus was still sitting on her deckchair, surrounded by fresh piles of rubble. She invited them inside to drink coffee and they sat there round the vast table that Matthieu now knew so well. Libero had joined them. Claudie spoke and Matthieu heard his mother speaking in the language he did not understand although he knew it was his own, she took Gavina Pintus's hand. The latter shook her head in refusal and Claudie leaned towards her and went on talking without Matthieu being able to do anything other than guess at what she was saying,

"You took my son in, as if he were your own, now it's our turn. No-one's offering you charity. It's our turn,"
and she went on talking with tireless force of conviction until Matthieu understood, on seeing Libero's face light up into a smile, that she had obtained what she had come for.

At first there was a festive air about Bernard Gratas's way of the cross. Matthieu and Libero were back in Paris at work on their dissertations when he began organising poker games every week in the back room at the bar. It is highly unlikely that Bernard Gratas would have taken such an initiative on his own. It had doubtless been suggested to him by someone who needed to remain anonymous but had plainly grasped that here was a sucker whose dearest and most urgent desire was to be fleeced. These games met with great success once word got round in the area that Gratas was a player as terrible as he was rash, and one, what's more, who believed that poker was a game of chance and that one's luck always turned in the end. He started to smoke cigarillos, but this did not help him at all, any more than the dark glasses that he now wore by day as well as by night. He lost money like a lord, with a style that extended to offering rounds of drinks to his executioners. One day, without any advance warning, his wife and children and the old woman disappeared. When Marie-Angèle heard the news she called on him to offer her sympathy and found him at the bar in a state of remarkable elation. He confirmed that his wife had left, taking all the furniture with her. He was sleeping on a mattress, which she had grudgingly agreed to leave behind for him. Marie-Angèle was about to make a few suitable remarks when he observed roundly that it was the best thing that had ever happened to him, he was finally rid of a scold and three brats who were as thick as they were ungrateful, not to mention the old woman who, before declining into senility and incontinence, had made his life a misery by doling out generous helpings of spite, being quite unbelievably wicked, so wicked that he suspected her of secretly relishing the fact that she was now senile and was thus assured of being a real pain in the arse to the end of her days without anyone being able to reproach her for it, and he had no doubt at all that she would live to be a hundred, she was as tough as old boots, he had spent years dreaming about an accident in the home or euthanasia, without ever saying a word, stoically enduring a life he wouldn't wish on his worst enemy, but that was all over and now it was time to live, he had no intention of missing out on this, he would be able to express his true personality at last, the one he'd always kept hidden deep inside him, out of weariness, out of disgust, out of cowardice, but he was through with knuckling under, he was being reborn, and he told Marie-Angèle that it was thanks to her that he now felt at home there, surrounded by dear friends, his wife could snuff it for all he cared, that was no concern of his now, he'd won the right to be selfish, won it the hard way, and never, ever, had he felt so happy, for now he was truly happy, he kept on repeating, with evident and almost pathological sincerity, fixing on Marie-Angèle a look so overcome with gratitude that she was afraid he might hurl himself at her and hug her in his arms, which he was obviously restraining himself from doing, contenting himself with saying thank you but without being able to admit that he was above all grateful to her for having given birth to Virginie, with whom he had for the past few weeks been having the affair that had finally made a happy man of him. And never has happiness been more ostentatious. Bernard Gratas was forever laughing loudly at the slightest provocation, he was bursting with energy, constantly rushing back and forth between the counter and the main bar area without ever showing the least sign of fatigue or drunkenness, even though he had now started drinking like a fish, he heaped totally misplaced marks of affection on his customers and lost money with visible delight, there was something profoundly disturbing about the spectacle of his euphoria, it was as if it could only be the symptom of an appalling psychic sickness, and it inspired fears that it might be contagious. The more attentive and friendly Bernard Gratas appeared, the more people turned away from him in distaste, without his seeming to be aware of it, so resolved was he now to live in a world ruled only by illusion. But, alas, it seems the rule of illusion can never be perfect, and even a man like Bernard Gratas must have vaguely sensed that none of all this was real, as he staggered beneath the weight of a certain knowledge that he could neither eradicate nor put into words, but could only run away from by parading his happiness with grotesque, desperate stubbornness, and he could not understand why he sometimes woke up in the night, his heart thumping with anguish because on that day in June, after he had asked Virginie to come and live with him, she had replied with a disdainful shrug of her shoulders that he was off his head and she never wanted to see him again, after which she went and sat on the terrace in the sun and ordered a cold drink from him, which he served without saying a word. The very thing he had striven to escape from had just caught up with him and broken him. Virginie threw him an irritated glance.

"Don't pull that face. You look ridiculous."

He went on with his work normally for several days, as if carried along by an absurd momentum, and then one evening, at apéritif time, when the bar was full of customers, he burst into tears and paraded his unhappiness, just as he had done his happiness, with the same shameless candour, loudly evoking, between sobs, the perfection of Virginie's naked body, and her sulky queen's inscrutable fixed stare as he sweated away at coming in and out of her with all his might without ever managing to extract so much as a sigh from her, as if she were merely a witness to a scene she was following with keen attention, but which only concerned her vaguely, and he wept as he recalled how the more fervently he loved her, the more fixed and hard her gaze became from beneath those long eyelashes that betrayed not a flicker and he felt himself both humiliated and mesmerised by this look of hers that transformed him into a laboratory animal without his arousal growing any the less, quite the contrary, he said, sniffing noisily, he was more and more aroused, and in the bar the first murmurs of disapproval began to be heard, someone shouted at him to get a grip on himself, and then to shut his trap, but he could not be quiet, he was now out of reach of shame, his face glistening with tears and snot and, as he came out with specific, distasteful details, talking about the way Virginie, without taking her eyes off him, would press the palm of her hand against his back and draw her outstretched middle finger slowly down his spine, while fixing him now with a kind of sorrowful contempt that he recognised every time with terror, knowing that it would soon be impossible for him to stop himself coming and, as the appalled assembled company continued to follow the descent of this indecent middle finger, guessing all too well at its inexorable destination, and was already resigning itself to enduring the detailed description of a Bernard Gratas orgasm, Vincent Leandri went up to him, slapped him twice and dragged him outside by the arm. Bernard Gratas was now on his knees on the asphalt and no longer weeping. He looked at Vincent.

"I've lost everything. I've screwed up my whole life."

Vincent did not reply. He was trying to mobilise all his faculties for compassion, but still wanted to hit him. He offered him a handkerchief.

"You've slept with her as well. I know you have. How could she do this?"

Vincent squatted down beside him.

"If you thought you and Virginie were a couple, you're a bigger fool than I thought you were. Stop boring the pants off everyone with your tale. Pull yourself together."

Bernard Gratas shook his head.

"I've screwed up my whole life."

In the end Libero found reasons of his own for loathing Paris which owed nothing to Matthieu. And thus it was that every evening and every morning, side by side in a crowded carriage on Line 4, both of them would be sunk in irremediable bitterness, although this had different significance for each of them. For Libero had at first believed he had gained admission to the very throbbing heart of learning, as an initiate who has triumphed in tests beyond the comprehension of common mortals, he could not set foot inside the great hall of the Sorbonne without feeling overcome by the apprehensive pride that signals the presence of the gods. For at his back came his illiterate mother, his brothers, who were tillers of the land and shepherds, and all his ancestors, prisoners of the pagan darkness of Barbaggia, all aquiver with joy in the depths of their graves. He had faith in the eternity of things eternal, in their steadfast nobility, which is inscribed upon the monumental pediment of a pure and lofty heaven. Then he lost his faith. He was taught ethics by an extraordinarily verbose and amiable young graduate of the Ecole Normale Supérieure, who discussed texts with a nonchalance so brilliant it was nauseating, bombarding his students with decisive observations about absolute evil that would not have been disavowed by a village priest, albeit decked out with a generous helping of references and quotations, which did nothing to compensate for their conceptual emptiness or to conceal their absolute triviality. And, to crown it all, what this wallowing in moralism was simply designed to serve was an utterly cynical ambition, it was palpably obvious that for him the university was merely a necessary but insignificant stage on a road that would lead him to the crowning glory of appearing on television talk shows where, in the company of similar creatures, he would publicly debase the name of philosophy, before the delighted gaze of uncultured and gleeful presenters, for Libero was no longer in any doubt that the media and commerce had now taken the place of thought, and he was like a man who, after unbelievable striving, has just won a fortune in a currency that is no longer valid. It is true that the attitude of this Normalien was not typical of that of the other teachers, who fulfilled their task with an austere integrity that won them Libero's respect. He had boundless admiration for the doctoral student who, every Thursday from six to eight p.m., dressed in beige corduroy trousers and a bottle green jacket with gilded buttons that looked as if it had come from a Stasi surplus shop and bore witness to his indifference to material goods, would comment imperturbably on Book Gamma of the *Metaphysics* of Aristotle in front of a meagre audience of persistent and attentive students of ancient Greek philosophy. But the atmosphere of devotion that prevailed in the dusty lecture room on Staircase C to which they had been relegated could not conceal the extent of their rout, they were all losers, beings who had failed to adapt, and would soon be incomprehensible, the survivors of a sly apocalypse which had decimated the ranks of their fellow students and brought low the temples of the divinities they worshipped, the light of which had once shone round the world. For a long time Libero felt affection for his comrades in misfortune. They were honourable men. Their shared defeat was their badge of honour. It ought to be possible to act as if nothing had happened, to continue leading a life resolutely behind the times, completely devoted to the veneration of relics that have been profaned. Libero still believed the honourable nature of such a life was inscribed on the monumental pediment of a pure and lofty heaven and it mattered little that its existence was known to no-one. One must turn aside from those moral and political questions that are corrupted by the poison of topicality, and take refuge in the arid deserts of metaphysics, in the company of authors who were never likely to be tarnished by media attention. He decided to do his dissertation on Augustine. Matthieu, whose steadfast friendship often took the form of sycophantic approval, chose Leibniz and lost himself without conviction in the giddy labyrinths of the divine intellect, in the shadow of the unimaginable pyramid of possible worlds in which his hand, multiplied to infinity, finally made contact with Judith's cheek.

Libero read the four sermons on the fall of Rome, feeling as if he were performing an act of supreme resistance and also read *The City of God*, but as the nights drew in the last of his optimism became dissolved in the mist and rain that bore down on the damp pavements. Everything was sad and dirty, nothing was written in heaven but promises of storms and drizzle and his band of resistance fighters now became as loathsome as the conquerors, they were not villains but clowns and failures, and he the first among them, who had been trained to produce dissertations and commentaries as useless as they were irreproachable, for the world might still have need of Augustine and Leibniz, but it had no use at all for the wretched authors of critical commentaries and Libero was now filled with contempt for himself and for his teachers, scholars and philistines alike, as well as for his fellow pupils, beginning with Judith Haller, whom he reproached Matthieu for continuing to see, on the grounds that when she was not being stupid she was being pedantic, nothing escaped the furious outbursts of his contempt, not even Augustine, whom he could no longer abide, now he was certain he had understood him better than ever before. He now saw him as nothing more than an uncivilised barbarian who rejoiced in the fall of the Empire because it marked the arrival of the world of mediocrities and triumphant slaves, of which he was a part, his sermons were dripping with vengeful and perverse relish, there was the ancient world of gods and poets disappearing before his eyes, swamped by Christianity with its repellent cohort of ascetics and martyrs, and there was Augustine concealing his glee beneath hypocritical accents of wisdom and compassion that smacked of village priests. Libero finished his dissertation as best he could in such a state of moral exhaustion that continuing his studies had become impossible. When he learned that Bernard Gratas had completed his descent into destitution with a fine flourish, he knew that a unique opportunity beckoned and told Matthieu that they absolutely must take on the management of the bar. Matthieu was quite naturally all in favour. When they reached the village, at the beginning of summer, Bernard Gratas had just informed Marie-Angèle that, because of undeserved but consistent losses at poker, he would be unable to pay the management fee and the fresh slaps Vincent Leandri dealt him made no difference. Marie-Angèle received the news stoically. Having abandoned all hope of improving the situation, she went so far as to consider that, rather than resuming charge of the bar herself, she might leave its management to Gratas until September, so that he could pay her at least a part of what he owed her. Libero and Matthieu came to see her and offered their services. She freely recognised that it would be hard for them to do worse than their predecessors. But where could they find the money? She trusted them, she had known them since they were children and knew they had no intention of cheating her, but the fact was that she had to eat and she absolutely had to be paid in advance. By going and making his case to his brothers and sisters, Libero managed to put together two thousand euros. Matthieu announced his plan one evening in July at the family supper table. Claudie and Jacques laid down their spoons. His grandfather went on drinking his soup with meticulous care.

"Do you think we're going to give you money so you can abandon your studies and manage a bar? Do you seriously think that?"

Matthieu attempted to make his case, offering arguments he judged to be irrefutable, but his mother cut him off brutally.

"Hold your tongue."

She was pale with fury.

"Leave the table at once. I want you out of my sight."

He felt humiliated but obeyed her without a word. He rang his sister to angle for her support but could not get her to understand. Aurélie burst out laughing.

"What a load of nonsense. Did you really think Maman was going to jump for joy?"

Again Matthieu tried to defend himself. She would not listen.

"It's time you grew up. You're starting to be a bore."

He went to see Libero to give him the bad news and they got gloomily drunk together. When Matthieu woke up, about noon the next day, with a bad headache, due as much to despair as to drink, his grandfather was seated at his bedside. Matthieu sat up painfully. Marcel was looking at him with unaccustomed benevolence.

"So you want to settle down here and look after the bar, do you, my boy?"

Matthieu assented with a vague nod of his head.

"Here's what I'll do. I'll pay the fee and the rent for this year and I'll pay it again next year. After that you'll get nothing, nothing at all, not a centime. That, my boy, will give you two years to prove your worth."

Matthieu flung his arms around his neck. The week that followed was apocalyptic. Claudie made a terrible scene. She accused Marcel of spite and sabotage in aggravating circumstances with malice aforethought, he was only helping his grandson because he hated him and wanted to see him ruin his life, purely for the satisfaction of proving he hadn't been mistaken about him, and as for the other young idiot, who was over the moon about it, he understood nothing and was cheerfully hurling himself into the abyss, like the stupid little idiot that he was, and in vain Marcel protested his good faith, it did no good, she pilloried him, yelling that one way or another he would pay for his infamous conduct, and she said the same to Marie-Angèle, turning up at her house without warning and creating a scandal by asking her if it was to console herself for having given birth to a whore that she was setting out to lead other people's children astray, but that did no good and in the end Claudie calmed down and halfway through July Matthieu and Libero took over the bar, having magnanimously engaged Gratas to do the washing up. Libero walked over to behind the counter. He examined the colourful row of bottles, the sinks, the cash register, and felt he belonged there. This was a valid currency. Everyone understood the point of it and had faith in it. That was what gave it its value and no other chimerical value system on earth, as in heaven, could be opposed to it. Libero no longer wanted to resist. And, while Matthieu was fulfilling his life's dream by laying waste with savage joy to the lands of his past with fire and the sword, and instantly erasing the messages of support and regret that Judith persisted in sending him, be happy, when shall I see you again? don't forget me, as if he could thus expel her from his dream, Libero had long since ceased dreaming. He admitted defeat and was now giving his assent, a sorrowful, total, desperate assent, to the world's stupidity.

"You, see yourself for what you are.
For it is necessary for the fire to come"

The mountains hide the open sea, however, rearing up with all their inert mass against Marcel and his steadfast dreams. From the courtyard at the primary school in Sartène all he can make out is the headland at the end of the gulf that reaches deep into the land where the sea looks like a vast lake, peaceful and insignificant. He does not need to see the sea in order to dream, Marcel's dreams are nourished neither by contemplation nor by metaphor but by struggle, waging an unceasing fight against the inertia of things that all resemble one another, as if, beneath the apparent diversity of their shapes, they were all made of the same heavy, viscous, malleable stuff, even the water in the rivers is murky and on the empty beaches the lapping of the waves gives off a sickly smell of marshland, one needs to struggle not to become inert oneself, allowing oneself to be slowly engulfed, as if by a quicksand, and still Marcel wages his unceasing battle against the forces unleashed within his own body, against the demon striving to pin him down on his bed, his mouth full of ulcers, his tongue eaten away by the flow of acidic juices, as if a gimlet had gouged out a well of exposed flesh within his chest and stomach, he fights against despair at being perpetually pinned to a bed moist with sweat and blood, against time wasted, he fights against his mother's weary look, against his father's silent resignation, as he waits for the moment when he will regain both his strength and the right to be there in the courtyard at the primary school in Sartène, his view blocked by the barrier of the mountains. He is the first and only one of his brothers and sisters to continue his studies into secondary school and neither the demons within his body nor the inertia of things will stop him continuing with them as far as the teacher training college and well beyond, for he has no desire to be a teacher, he has no desire to dish out useless lessons to poor, dirty children whose terrified gaze would drive him back to the disarray of his own childhood, he has no desire to leave his village only to bury himself in another desperately similar village, perched like a tumour on the soil of an island where nothing changes, for the truth is that nothing there does change, nor will it ever change. His brother, Jean-Baptiste, has been sending money from Indochina and has bought his parents a house large enough for all the members of the family to stay there in the summer with-out being obliged to sleep squeezed up against one another like livestock in a cowshed. Marcel has his own room, but the layers of peeling skin still cling to his father's dry lips and his mother's brow is still knitted by the deep, rectilinear furrow of mourning, they look neither younger nor older than fifteen years ago, just after the world ended, and when he studies his own figure in the mirror he has the feeling that he was born like this, thin and shaky, and that his childhood has set its cruel stamp on him from which nothing can free him. Jean-Baptiste kept changing in the photographs he used to send because he lived in a part of the world where the passage of time still left tangible traces, he would grow visibly fatter, then, just as brutally became thin, as if his body were being constantly upset by the powerful, anarchic ebb and flow of life itself, he would pose at attention with an impeccably trim uniform and hair, or else half undressed, with his kepi on the back of his head, with a background of unfamiliar vegetation, in the company of other soldiers and girls dressed in silk, his face was bloated by fat and plenty, or hollowed out by weariness, debauchery or fever, but always the same mocking, gleeful expression could be read there, he adopted the swagger of a pimp and Marcel no longer admired him, he envied him the way he so openly relished the wealth he did not deserve. Everything he saw of his brother had become intolerable to him, his evident taste for whores, his imposing build, his leanness and his fatness, the insolence of his attitude, even his generosity, for all that money could not have been saved out of the pay he received as a sergent-chef, and must certainly be derived from vile trafficking, in lucre, opium, or human flesh. When Jean-Baptiste came back to the village for Jeanne-Marie's wedding he was still just as corpulent as on the day of his departure and his face was still lit up by the juvenile expression of the man he had become over there, in those inconceivable lands where

83

the sea foam was translucent and shone in the sunlight like a spray of diamonds, he was surrounded by his wife and children, his sleeves and kepi were decorated with the golden anchor, the badge of the colonial army, but the toxic influence of his native land caused him to revert to what he had never ceased to be, a clumsy, uneducated peasant whom fate had catapulted into a world he did not merit, and neither the cases of champagne he had ordered for his young sister's wedding nor his ludicrous plan for opening a hotel in Saigon when he left the service would make a whit of difference. They were all wretched peasants, born of a world that had long since ceased to exist, but which clung to the soles of their shoes like mud, the viscous and malleable stuff they themselves were formed of, which they carried with them everywhere they went, whether to Marseille or Saigon, and Marcel knows he is the only one who can really escape from it. The *beignets* were too dry and covered in a layer of hardened sugar, the tepid blandness of the champagne left a taste of ashes in the mouth and the men sweated under the summer sun, but Jeanne-Marie radiated a timid joy, and the veil of satin and white lace that emphasised the oval of her face gave her the grace of an antique maiden of Judaea. She danced, clinging with all her might to her husband's shoulders while he wore a grave smile, as if he already knew he would not survive the new war that even now lay in wait for them all. For beyond the barrier of the mountains, beyond the sea, there is a world in turmoil and it is over there, far away from them, without them,

84

that their lives and their future are once again being determined and that is how it has always been. But the hubbub of this world gets lost at sea, long before reaching them and the reverberations that come Marcel's way are so distant and confused that he cannot bring himself to take them seriously and in the school courtyard at Sartène he shrugs his shoulders with contempt when his friend Sebastien Colonna tries to get him to share his enthusiasm for the ideas of Charles Maurras and talks about the dawn of a new age and the rebirth of the *patrie*, which, thanks to the Jews and Bolsheviks, has gone to rack and ruin, and Marcel says, What on earth are you talking about? You've never seen a Jew or a Bolshevik in your life! shrugging his shoulders with contempt because he does not see how anyone could get fired up like this over the foggy unreality of such abstract notions. What causes Marcel's pulses to race is the concrete and exquisite thought of soon doing his military service, his level of education will allow him to become an officer, he can already picture the gilded line of his officer cadet's stripe and when, in a moment of jocularity during the wedding, Jean-Baptiste, his mouth crammed with *beignets*, saluted him with mock solemnity before ruffling his hair with a laugh, as if he were a ten-year-old, Marcel could not restrain feelings of secret joy over this, which not even the declaration of war took the shine off. Jeanne-Marie came back and settled in the house in the village with Jean-Baptiste's wife and children. They waited for daily letters from the Maginot Line that spoke of boredom, frustration and victory, Jeanne-Marie's young husband wrote that he missed her, and that, as the nights grew cold, he was thinking about the warmth of her skin against his own, he was impatient for the Germans to attack so that he could defeat them and return to her, he wrote to say he swore he'd never leave her, no, never, when all this was merely a distant and glorious memory, he'd never leave her. Time passed and he wrote more things to her than he would ever have dared to say to her face, even in whispers, he spoke of her belly arched beneath his caresses, of her thighs, of her breasts, whose whiteness was to die for, and again of the imminent victory, as if the glory of his wife's body were mingled and even confused with that of the country he was defending, every day he became more exalted, explicit and warlike, and Jeanne-Marie was thrilled by his letters and prayed to God to bring him home soon, with no fear of her wish not being granted. In March 1940 Marcel, having sworn to the army doctor that he had never had the slightest problems with his health, finally leaves his sister, his village and his parents to join a unit of officer cadets in an artillery regiment in Draguignan. Once across the sea, the demon of the ulcer seems to be disabled, deprived of its power to do harm, and for the first time in his life Marcel enjoys a vigour whose existence he had never suspected, he behaves like the diligent pupil he has always been and is deaf to all the rest, failing to hear the roar of the panzers, the smashed trees in the Ardennes forests, the clamour of the flight from Paris and the tears of humiliation, all dreams of victory swept aside by a tempest of rout, he does not hear Philippe Pétain's voice speaking of honour and armistice, and as the first letter written by Jean-Baptiste from a German stalag arrives at the village, as well as the telegram informing Jeanne-Marie that she is a widow at twenty-five, Marcel finally hears, without being able to believe it, the unit commander informing the men in his platoon that they will never be commissioned, that they have all been assigned to Maréchal Pétain's Chantiers de Jeunesse programme and grasps that all that he will be is a glorified boy scout singing the Maréchal's praises and a burning acid rips through his stomach and chest, bringing him to his knees in the midst of his comrades, and in front of the unit commander who watches him vomiting blood into the dust. On leaving hospital, after being discharged, he goes and settles in Marseille at the home of one of his older sisters and spends whole days lying on his bed, lulled by resentment and nausea, without being able to bring himself to go home to the village, to return to its unchanging embrace of anguish and mourning and he delays his departure, desperately clinging to this vast, dirty city, as if it were to be his salvation. He is convinced that life has run up an immense debt to him, which it can only settle if he remains here, for he knows that once he sets foot on his native soil, all accounts will be cancelled, the insults and prejudice, the compensations, and existence will no longer owe him anything. He is waiting for something to happen and he wanders up and down the streets of this city whose vastness and dirtiness frighten him, he glances uneasily towards the harbour, trying to resist the poisonous seduction of homesickness and he stops up his ears, for he is afraid of hearing sweet and beloved voices from beyond the sea, calling on him to return to the limbo he came from. Sebastien Colonna has joined him and every day dozens of his compatriots arrive in Marseille, looking for work there. On the recommendation of an uncle of Sebastien's, Marcel has been taken on at the Société Genérale bank. But the weeks were going by and still those debts had not been settled. So was this how life settled its debt? Was this how life compensated him for not being an officer, by forcing him to immerse himself in account books that made him choke with boredom, his only permitted respite from them being listening to Sebastien's interminable harangues on the merits of national revolution, praising the wisdom of God, and the way He helped men to derive edifying and salutary lessons from the worst catastrophes, extolling sacrifice and resignation, for what France needed was brutal medicine to purge herself of the poison that infected her – was this how life did it? So wasn't life hounding him, with its repeated contempt, straight into the arms of the whore he had decided to accost, both so as to satisfy his desire for knowledge and to seek solace? She had dark, compassionate eyes that shone with a deceptive gentleness that quickly vanished once she was alone with him, and no glimmer now lit up the look she focused on him as he performed his ablutions in a cracked and grimy bidet, she stared at him pitilessly and he trembled with shame, anticipating the bitterness of what he was about to learn and no longer hoping for solace. He climbed after her into sheets that smelled of mould where to the very end he had to tolerate the affront of her impassiveness. He felt the heat at the place where their bellies met and mingled like the cloacae of reptiles, he felt the clamminess of her breasts pressing against his chest, her legs against his own, intolerable images arose in Marcel's mind, he was an animal, a great voracious, shuddering bird, plunged up to its neck into the entrails of a rotting carcase, for she maintained the obscene impassiveness of a carcase, her dead eyes staring at the ceiling, and in the places where their skins touched, at each point of contact, fluids were being exchanged, transparent lymph, intimate humours, as if, in a hideous meta-morphosis, his body were going to retain the imprint of this woman's body for ever, although he would never see her again and did not know her name, and he got up abruptly to dress and leave. He emerged, panting, into the street, alien blood flowed in his veins, the sweat trickling down onto his eyelids no longer smelled the same and he spat on the ground because he did not recognise the taste of his own saliva. He spent weeks anxiously examining his body, every tiny pimple, every rash, feeling he was doomed to get skin infections, thrush, syphilis, gonorrhoea, but whatever name were given to the illness that lay in wait for him, that would only be the outward form in which the malady that had him in its grip would declare itself, irremediably, and he pestered the doctors every week until the day arrived when the German army invaded the Free Zone and forced him to abandon his self-obsession. Sebastien Colonna was horrified, fulminating against the Allies' recklessness and Hitler's treachery in not keeping his word, but his confidence in the paternal authority of the Maréchal was manifestly shaken, he was afraid he would be sent to do forced labour in a German factory and said to Marcel, We need to get away from here, we need to leave at once. But boats were no longer leaving the harbour. Sebastien learned from his uncle that a liner was due to leave for Bastia from Toulon in a few days' time. Marcel and he went there by bus. They saw columns of black smoke arising above the sea, all that was left of the scuttled French fleet was a mass of sheet metal and steel obstructing the harbour, the screaming German Stukas were dive bombing the rare ships that were trying to escape by threading their way between mines and anti-submarine nets, and Sebastien burst into tears. When the dire straits he himself was in eventually struck him as being at least as worthy of interest as the honour of the French navy, he explained to Marcel that it was essential for them to cross into the Italian occupation zone if they wanted to give themselves a chance of getting back home. Marcel replied that he had no money left for further travel and was going to go back to his sister in Marseille but Sebastien said no, this was out of the question, he had some money and would not abandon him, and thus Marcel learned that friendship is a mystery. They managed to reach Nice and were back in their village a week later. Now Jeanne-Marie's grief has begun to invade the house and hangs there like a fog that nothing will come and dispel. Everything is muted beneath a veil of silence so heavy that Marcel sometimes wakes up with a start, pining for the screaming bombs on Toulon harbour. He gets up to have a drink and finds his father standing in the kitchen, completely unmoving, with a fixed stare and Marcel asks him, Papa, what are you doing here? but receives no reply other than a tilt of the head, which plunges him back into the endless silence. He looks at his father in terror, as he stands there in his rough woollen nightshirt, with his burned eyelids and lashes and his white lips and, despite the panic overcoming him, he cannot look away, he summons up all his strength, edges past him, takes the jug to help himself to water and goes back to bed, vowing never to get up again during the nights that follow, even if he is being tortured by thirst, for he knows he will find his father standing on the same spot, lost to the world, petrified in a woeful stupor, which death itself will not put an end to. Marcel would like to extricate himself from this strait-jacket of silence, he hears the great wind of rebellion blowing all about him and is waiting for its bloody squalls to rip the doors and windows off the house to let in fresh air. Sebastien Colonna recounts tales of parachute drops, assassinations with hand grenades, he tells how over in the Alta Rocca region, two Andreani cousins murdered an Italian before joining the maquis, and condemns these futile and criminal acts without realising that

Marcel does not share his disapproval and is already picturing himself taking up arms against the invader. In early February an unknown person began killing lone Italian soldiers, once a week, with relentless regularity. Their bodies would be found, lying in the mud, close to an overturned motorcycle, on mountain roads within a radius of a few miles from the village. They had been brought down by buckshot and sometimes finished off by having their throats cut with a knife, bled like pigs, some of them had been more or less undressed and all of them had been brutally stripped of their shoes. The shoes were nowhere to be found and it was this detail, innocuous in itself, that gave rise to respect and terror in people's minds, as if the assassin were indulging in a ritual all the more frightening because it was incomprehensible and there were mutterings that this was nothing to do with the maquis, it was the work of a mysterious partisan, a messenger of certain death, a pitiless loner, like the legendary Archangel of the Lord of hosts. With the exception of Sebastien Colonna, whose contempt for Italians was counterbalanced by his admiration for Mussolini and his visceral and passionate penchant for authority, all the young men in the village wanted to join the resistance, so that they, too, might become fearsome killers in the cause of justice. They could no longer tolerate inaction. They met to discuss what they could do, they considered liquidating traitors and collaborators and someone even mentioned Sebastien's name, but Marcel spoke warmly in his defence and reminded them that he had never harmed anybody. In the end they arranged a nocturnal rendezvous in the mountains with a combat unit and set off from the village at one o'clock in the morning, marching together through the chilly night, borne along by the enthusiasm of their youthful militancy, but when they had got past the school they heard the sound of feet marching in quick time, approaching from a few dozen yards up the hill, whereupon they fled down to the village again and scuttled back into their homes to watch out with thumping hearts for the passing of the Italian patrol, which they never saw because they had run away from the echo of their own footsteps flung back at them by the night's icy silence. They were crushed by shame. They carefully avoided one another, so as not to have to face up to their dishonour. In the spring the mystery killer was no longer heard of and no-one knew whether he had perished or had returned to his dwelling in heaven, there to await the Apocalypse. The mystery was only solved during the September uprising, which, for Marcel, amounted to a few comings and goings in the streets of the village, a useless rifle in his hand. Ange-Marie Ordioni came down from the shepherd's hut high above the forest of Vaddi Mali where he lived with his wife, leading the primitive life of a Stone Age hunter. He was shod in Italian lace-up boots and wore a military jacket from which he had removed the stripes and epaulettes. In the depths of winter his only pair of boots had begun to disintegrate, he was unable to mend them and had no money to buy himself new ones. It had seemed to him quite natural to help himself from the occupying forces, but it had taken him some time to find a pair that fitted him for, despite his caveman build, he had ridiculously small feet. One of the senior figures in the Front National yelled that he was an idiot and a madman and he ought to have him shot on the spot but Ange-Marie gave him a chilling look and remarked that he would do better to keep quiet. In the mountains you need good boots. The French forces arrived in the village, the auxiliary soldiers from North Africa laughed and drank, they sang in Arabic in the streets, Marcel stared in amazement at their shaven heads, the long pigtails of plaited hair that hung down the backs of their necks, the Saracen curvature of their knives, and Sebastien said to him, Feast your eyes on what our liberators look like, Moors and Negroes, it's always the same, to begin with the barbarians lend their services to the Empire, later on they hasten its downfall and destroy it. There'll be nothing left of us. A few weeks later the two of them were vomiting side by side on board the Liberty Ship taking them to Algiers through the storms. Upsurges of sea water as dense as mud washed away their defilement and froze them to the marrow. In Maison-Carrée, close to Algiers, a sous-officier sat at a desk, his nose buried in a dull register, and informed them of their respective postings with an indifferent air, and there was nothing to show that it was there, behind that desk, that reprieves and death sentences were being decided, for this was the irrevocable place of the parting of the ways, the place where, without appeal, the sheep were separated from the goats, the former to the left, the latter to the right, but nobody asked them to choose between the glory of dying in battle and a life of insignificance, and at the very moment when Sebastien Colonna learned the name of his infantry regiment, he was already embarking on his ineluctable trajectory towards the machine-gun bullets that had always been waiting for him at Monte Cassino. Marcel embraced him as a matter of course, not knowing that all he would ever see of him again was his name, carved in letters of gold by unknown hands on a monument to the dead, as if marble were less perishable than human flesh, and he boarded a train for Tunis. On arrival he learned that he was being sent back with his battery to Casablanca to be trained in operating American anti-aircraft guns and he gave up trying to understand the logic of military postings. The train set off towards the west, hugging the coastline on a long journey that lasted three weeks. He was stretched out beside his comrades in goods wagons with their floors covered in warm straw on which he spent the best part of his time dozing, only rousing himself from his torpor to play cards or to watch the sad passing of plains and silent towns, not one of which lived up to the promise of his dreams, once more the sea lapped against lacklustre shorelines and no trace remained of the marvellous tales that peopled the history books, neither the fire of Baal, nor Scipio's African legions, there was not one Numidian knight besieging the walls of Cirta to restore Sophonisba's kiss to Massinissa after she had been stolen from him, both the walls and the men who had laid siege to them had returned to dust and nothingness together, for marble and flesh are equally subject to decay, at Bône all that remained of the cathedral beneath whose vault Augustine had preached and where his last breath was drowned by the clamour of the Vandals, was a waste land, covered in yellow plants and battered by the wind. He moved into his billet at Casablanca, firmly resolved to redeem himself from his indolence and become a proper soldier, but the Americans were not delivering the anti-aircraft guns and the wait soon became so unbearable that he almost went back to the brothel. He could not bring himself to believe that at this time, when the future of the world was at stake, he had once more been condemned to tedium, and the vastness of the Atlantic brought him no consolation. After a month he heard that they were looking for officers in the service corps and immediately put in an application. If they refused him the satisfaction of fighting, at least he could become what he had always wanted to be. He felt happy at last and remained so until the colonel summoned him to rebuke him for his shameful conduct in unbelievably violent terms, he foamed at the mouth, he banged his fist on his desk, you're nothing but a little shit heap, Antonetti, a double-dyed coward, and Marcel, distraught, stammered in vain, but, you see, mon colonel, mon colonel, and the colonel bellowed, service corps officer? the service corps? repeating the words "service corps", as if this were an unspeakable obscenity that soiled his mouth, so you're scared of fighting, is that it? You'd rather sit there counting kilos of potatoes and pairs of socks? You bastard! You little bastard! And Marcel swore to him that he lived only for fighting but that he had always wanted to become an officer and this had seemed like an opportunity to be seized, but the colonel did not calm down, if you wanted to be an officer you should have come to see me, an artillery officer, sir! an honourable officer! I would have assigned you to a platoon, but the service corps? The service corps, God dammit? Not one of my men will end up in the service corps, do you understand! Now piss off before I knock your block off! Marcel went out with his stomach on fire, all his hopes ruthlessly swept aside once more, and all he could do was continue to wait for the anti-aircraft guns, which still did not come, until in the end he was posted to the staff of a lieutenant in the service corps without the colonel or anyone else seeing anything at all paradoxical or scandalous in this. He arrived back in France with the lieutenant at the end of 1944 and they made their way slowly northwards several hundred miles behind the front line. Marcel took care of the paperwork and made vile coffee. He never heard the clash of arms. Just once, at Colmar, a few hundred yards from the vehicle he was driving, a stray shell landed, throwing up dust and rubble. Marcel stopped. He looked around him at the town in ruins which no shell could do more to destroy. For several minutes there was a pleasant buzzing in his ears. He turned to the lieutenant and asked him if he was alright and dusted off his sleeve with the flat of his hand, with a little frown, and this was his only feat of arms, the one thing that might help him to think the war had not held him completely at arm's length. And now the war is over and he is back at the village in the bosom of his family. He lets himself be embraced by his father, who hugs him to himself along with Jean-Baptiste, relaxes his embrace and then draws them to himself again, as if unable to believe that neither of his sons has been taken from him. Jean-Baptiste is radiant and has grown terribly fat. He has spent the last three years of the war on a farm in Bavaria managed by four sisters, he winks whenever he talks about them, after first making sure his wife is not looking his way and Marcel is afraid he wants to get him on his own so he can come out with a flood of smutty confidences. He has no desire to hear these. He is twenty-six. He will never again see the courtyard of the primary school at Sartène, he is too old and, when he takes a look at his hands, he has the feeling that they will soon disintegrate like hands made of sand. In Paris, where she went to look for Jean-Baptiste, Jeanne-Marie has met a young man, much younger than herself, a resistance fighter back from deportation, and announces that she is going to marry him. She is already irremediably worn out by grief and knows it, but she behaves as if she still believed in the future. Marcel resents her making such vain and ludicrous efforts to appear full of life, it pains him to see his sister acting out this masquerade of forgetting, he refuses to pretend to be joyful and all the time she is busying herself with preparations for the wedding he resists her with a stubborn and contemptuous silence. But in the church, as she walks up the aisle to where André Degorce is waiting, slim and youthful in his Saint-Cyr military college uniform, she stops for a moment and turns to Marcel, giving him a childlike smile, and, as if in spite of himself, he can only smile back. This is no charade, she is neither demeaning herself in an act of renunciation nor making a mockery, because the boundless capacity for love that she carries within herself will always preserve her from such things. Marcel feels ashamed of his own sharpness and cynicism and, in that bright morning he feels shame all over again, shame at his own craven heart, his heart filled with darkness, and beside André he feels ashamed of having been such a paltry warrior, ashamed of his contemptible good fortune, ashamed, too, at not even being able to rejoice in it, he views André with jealous respect and is ashamed to be receiving him into this wretched village, all the wedding guests fill him with shame, the Colonna household, still in mourning, and the Susini family, who have allowed their half-wit daughter, pregnant with her umpteenth bastard child, to come with them and Ange-Marie Ordioni, crimson with pride, hugging to his bemedalled chest the big baby boy his wife has just given birth to amid the filth of their shepherd's hut, he is ashamed of his own parents, of Jean-Baptiste's obscene and superabundant vitality and of himself, bearing within his breast that craven heart filled with darkness. He watches his sister dancing in André's arms. The children run about between the rickety tables. Ange-

Marie Ordioni gets his son to suck a finger he had dipped in his glass of rosé. Marcel hears the laughter and the accordion playing out of tune, Jean-Baptiste's stentorian voice. He sits in the sun beside his mother, who takes his hand and shakes her head sadly. She alone does not seem happy to see life resuming its course. For how, indeed, could life be resuming its course when it had not even begun?

"What man makes man destroys"

In August, before she left for Algeria, Aurélie came to spend a couple of weeks at the village with the man who was still sharing her life and was quite astonished to encounter an upsurge of seething and chaotic vitality there that spilled over into everything, but manifestly had its source in her brother's bar. A diverse and cheerful clientele was to be found there, a mixture of regulars, young people from the neighbouring villages and tourists of all nationalities, amazingly brought together in a festive and bibulous communion which, against all expectations, was not troubled by any discord. It was as if this were the place chosen by God for an experiment in the reign of love upon earth and even the locals, normally so quick to complain of the slightest type of pollution, uppermost among which must be counted the very existence of their fellow human beings, wore the fixed and blissful smiles of the elect. Bernard Gratas, returned victorious from his season in hell, now seemed touched by the breath of the all-conquering Spirit. He had been the beneficiary of a lightning promotion that had propelled him straight from the purgatory of washing up to the manufacture of sandwiches, a task he performed with good humour and alacrity. Four waitresses moved back and forth across the main bar area and onto the terrace, graciously bearing dishes, behind the counter an older woman seated on a stool looked after the till, a young man who accompanied himself on the guitar sang Corsican, English, French and Italian songs, and when he embarked on a catchy tune, all the customers clapped along with enthusiasm. Matthieu and Libero devoted themselves to improving customer relations, moving from table to table to enquire after the wellbeing of their guests, taking repeat orders for rounds of drinks and tickling little children under the chin after treating them to an ice cream, and they were the masters of a perfect world, a blessed world, one that flowed with milk and honey. Even Claudie had to face facts and observed with a sigh,

"Perhaps he was made for this,"
she looked at her son radiating happiness as he moved from table to table, and said again,

"It's what makes him happy that counts, isn't it?"
and Aurélie had no desire to upset her by admitting that Matthieu infuriated her beyond belief and that she saw nothing more in his happiness than the triumph of a spoilt child, a snotty little brat, who by dint of tears and screams has finally obtained the toy he wanted. She watched him playing with his toy in front of a captive audience and flaunting his delight, and there was a real danger that the exasperation it provoked in her would be neither deep nor lasting, since it arose neither from disappointed love, nor even

from anger, but was simply the prelude to a terminal form of indifference, the boy she had been so fond of and had so often comforted had slowly changed into a being with no breadth of interests, whose world was bounded by the horizon of his own trivial desires and Aurélie knew that, once she had got the measure of these, he would become a total stranger to her. Before going away she had come to take a fond farewell of her family, her grandfather in particular, and spend time with them. Every evening after dinner she witnessed Matthieu giving his performance, for it had apparently become obligatory to call in at the bar and have a drink there with the family, Matthieu would come and sit at their table, and talk about his plans for special events during the winter, the schemes he and Libero had devised for getting supplies of charcuterie, the accommodation for the waitresses, and the man who was sharing Aurélie's life at that time, and would do so for several months more, seemed to find all this of great interest, asking pertinent questions, and offering his opinion, as if it were essential for him to win Matthieu's affection, unless, as Aurélie was beginning to suspect, he was basically an idiot who was delighted to have encountered another idiot with whom he could feel at ease making idiotic remarks of all kinds. But at once she reproached herself for the unkindness of this attitude, the ease with which love was suddenly changing into contempt, and regretted having a churlish heart. She had nothing against bar managers, sandwiches and waitresses, and would not have passed any judgement on

Matthieu's choices if she had believed them to be sincere and considered, but she had no time either for play-acting or denial and Matthieu was behaving as if he must cut himself off from his past, he spoke with a contrived accent that had never been his own, an accent all the more ludicrous because on occasion he would lose it halfway through a sentence before blushing and correcting himself, to pick up the thread of the grotesque drama of his assumed identity from which the slightest idea, the tiniest evidence of intellect were excluded as dangerous elements. And Libero himself, whom Aurélie had always regarded as a thoughtful and intelligent boy, seemed resolved to follow the same path, being content to respond with a vaguely interrogative onomatopoeic noise when she told him she was going to spend the following year between the University of Algiers and Annaba, where she would be taking part in excavations on the site of Hippo with a team of French and Algerian archaeologists, as if the Saint Augustine, to whose writings he had just devoted a year of his life, were not worth a further second of his attention. Aurélie had given up talking to them about anything that really mattered to her and every evening, when she had reached the limit of what she could endure by way of singing, laughter and nonsense, she would get up from the table and say to her grandfather,

"Shall we go for a little stroll?"
and, to make it clear,

"Just the two of us?"

in case it had occurred to anybody else to join them, and they would walk together along the road leading up towards the mountain, Marcel took his granddaughter's arm, they left the sounds of merriment and the lights behind them, and sat down for a moment beside the fountain under the vast, starry August night sky. It was the first time Aurélie had been invited to join an international cooperative project and she was eager to start work. Her parents were concerned about her safety. The man who was sharing her life at that time was concerned about the durability of their relationship. Matthieu was concerned about nothing. Her grandfather viewed her as an enchantress, single-handedly capable of hoisting up vanished worlds from the abysses of dust and oblivion that had engulfed them and, in her moments of enthusiasm, when she had just embarked on her studies, that had been how she dreamed of herself. She had since become humbler and more serious. She knew that life cannot exist far from human eyes and strove to be one of those pairs of eyes that save life from extinction. But her churlish heart sometimes whispered to her that this was not true, all she brought into the light was dead things, she breathed no life into them, on the contrary, it was her own life that was slowly allowing itself to be invaded through and through by death, and Aurélie huddled close to her grandfather in the darkness. When the time came for her to leave she embraced him with all her might, then embraced all the rest of her family, trying to be even-handed in her affection. Matthieu said to her,

"Well, don't you think it's good, what we've managed to do?" seeking her approval with such childish insistence that she could only answer him,

"Yes, it's very good. I'm very happy for you," and gave him another kiss. She returned to Paris with the man who was sharing her life at that time and a few days later he went with her to Orly airport where once again, as the day dawned, and after a night of love which he had wanted to be intense and solemn, there were embraces and kisses which Aurélie gave and received as well as she could. The Air France plane was almost empty. Aurélie tried to read but could not manage to do so. She could not sleep either. The sky was cloudless. When the plane flew over the Balearic Islands Aurélie pressed her face against the window and stared at the sea until the African coast appeared. At Algiers the men from national security, armed with automatic rifles, were waiting on the tarmac where the aircraft came to a standstill. She stepped down from the gangway trying not to look at them and climbed into a creaking bus that took her to the terminal. Indescribable chaos reigned at the border police controls. Three or four flights must have landed at the same time, including a Boeing 747 that had arrived from Montreal nine hours late, and the police were examining every passport offered to them with extreme care, losing themselves in protracted and melancholy contemplation of the visa before resigning themselves to awarding it a desultory impress from the liberating rubber stamp. When, after an hour, she reached the baggage reclaim point, she found all the luggage scattered here and there in the hall on a floor covered in cigarette stubs and was afraid she would not find hers. She had to show her stamped passport again, smile at impassive customs officers and pass through electronic gates before finding herself in the arrivals hall. Behind barriers a crowd of people were pressed together, watching the entrance. Aurélie's heart was thumping nervously, she had never felt so lost and alone, she longed to go back home at once and when she read her name written in capital letters on a sheet of paper being waved by an unknown hand, she had such a violent sense of relief that she found it hard to keep herself from weeping.

Libero had had no intention of making the same mistakes as his hapless predecessors. He knew he was as lacking in expertise as Matthieu when it came to managing a bar but was confident that his local knowledge and a minimum of common sense would enable them to avoid another debacle. He spoke of the future like a visionary and Matthieu listened to him as if his were the voice of prophetic truth. They would have to moderate their ambitions, without abandoning them completely, there was no question of their offering a full restaurant service, that was hard labour and financially a bottomless pit, but they would offer their customers light meals, especially in summer, something simple, charcuterie, cheeses, maybe salads as well, without skimping on quality, people were prepared to pay for quality, that Libero was sure of, but as they must resign themselves to living in an age of mass tourism and give an equal welcome to hordes of people who were strapped for cash, there was no question of limiting themselves to luxury foods, they must also be prepared to serve crap at dirt-cheap prices and Libero knew how to resolve this formidable equation. His brother, Sauveur, and Virgile Ordioni would supply them with the best quality ham, cured over three years, and cheeses, really exceptional things, so very exceptional that anyone who tasted them would reach for his wallet weeping tears of gratitude, and, as for the rest, no point in burdening themselves with second-rate products, the rubbish that supermarkets sold in their local produce sections, packaged in rustic string bags decorated with a moor's head and perfumed in a factory with chestnut flour, much better quite frankly to go downmarket with no frills and serve Chinese pork carved in Slovakia that you could flog for next to nothing, but beware of treating people like idiots, you need to lay your cards on the table and present things so they understand the price differentials and don't get the impression they're being ripped off, the rubbish is a bargain, for quality you pay through the nose, honesty was absolutely essential in this, not only because it was an admirable virtue in itself but, above all, because it more or less fulfilled the function of a lubricant, the platters for sampling must be prepared in such a way that the customers can get an idea, taste it first and then you take an order afterwards, no, please try another piece, just to be sure, and this scrupulous honesty will be all the more rewarded because, whatever the final choice, the profit margins would be very much the same, they were going to fleece them all, all these suckers, poor and rich alike, irrespective of age or nationality, but fleece them openly, while at the same time pampering them, the manager of a bar must look after his customers, he couldn't spend all his time stuck there behind his till, like that halfwit Gratas, he must be on hand, pleasant, eager to please, so the crucial problem to be resolved was therefore one of waitresses. One evening Vincent Leandri took them to meet a friend who had managed various businesses on the mainland and now ran a bar down on the coast, it was smart and discreet although it could have earned him immediate conviction for aggravated procuring as Matthieu and Libero were quick to realise. He welcomed them with open arms and regaled them with champagne.

"You need someone reliable. And who knows about music."

He made a phone call and told them that Annie, an experienced waitress, who had worked for him in the past, might be interested. She arrived a quarter of an hour later, declared that Matthieu and Libero were sweet, drank almost a pint of champagne and assured them that she would be delighted to give them a hand. She would look after the till and manage the stock. For service in the main bar area they would need to find another waitress. Vincent's friend shook his head.

"Not one. One's not enough. You need three or four."

Libero pointed out that the bar was not very big, they didn't need so many girls and he didn't see how they could find the money to pay them. But Vincent's friend insisted.

"It's the summer. If you're not a couple of dopes you'll get a big crowd. If you want to stay open throughout the day as well as in the evening you'll need staff to do shifts. You can't make the same girl work eighteen hours a day, can you? And if it costs too much you could fire a couple of them. But then you'll be the ones that have to get up in the morning. In the evening you need girls. Two guys isn't good for trade. I know there are lots of poofters around, but you're not planning on opening a gay club, are you?"

He gave a hearty, coarse laugh. Libero was on the point of replying that he had no more intention of opening a gay club than a tart's bar but he was afraid of upsetting him.

"You get my meaning?"

Libero nodded.

"And whatever you do, don't screw the waitresses. Got it? People don't come to spend their dough at your place and watch you screwing the waitresses. You can screw the customers, but not the waitresses."

Annie agreed wholeheartedly, you could allow yourself to do lots of things in life, but if you were managing a bar you should never, absolutely never, screw the waitresses. Matthieu and Libero assured her that such an appalling notion had never crossed their minds.

They were surprised to note the following day that Annie, whose competence was in other respects irreproachable, seemed to have retained from her previous employment the curious custom of greeting each member of the male sex who crossed the threshold of the bar by stealthily but firmly stroking his balls. No-one escaped this grope. She went up to the new arrival, all smiles, and gave him two smacking kisses on both cheeks, while with her left hand, as if nothing were happening, she explored his crotch with lightly cupped fingers. The first one to pay the price for this odd habit was Virgile Ordioni who was coming in with his arms piled high with charcuterie. He turned crimson, gave a short laugh and remained standing there in the room not quite knowing what to do next. Matthieu and Libero had at first thought of asking Annie to try to show herself less immediately effusive, but nobody complained, quite the contrary, the men of the village put in several appearances at the bar over the course of the day, they even came there at normally quiet times, the hunters cut short their drives and Virgile made it a point of honour to come down from the mountain every day, if only for a coffee, so it came about that Matthieu and Libero held their peace, not without inwardly singing the perceptive Annie's praises, for in her immense wisdom she had penetrated the simplicity of the male psyche. Each evening, after closing the bar, they would set off on a recruiting campaign, touring the parties at campsites and on the beaches. They were looking for impecunious female students, doomed to the monotonous joys of sea bathing, who might be interested in seasonal work, and they were simply spoiled for choice. By the end of July they had found four waitresses. They also took on Pierre-Emmanuel Colonna, who had just passed his *baccalauréat* and was spending his summer holidays playing the guitar to his family, a committed audience but limited in size. He had no cause to regret turning professional, for not only was he a great hit with the clientele at the bar – whose aesthetic demands, it is true, were so easily satisfied that even the serenades bawled out by the likes of Virgile Ordioni when dead drunk were received with great acclaim – but from the very first evening his talent was rewarded by Annie who cornered him up against the billiard table after the bar had closed and kissed him on the mouth, while feeling him up vigorously, before granting him a night of such sheer licentiousness that it by far exceeded the most daring of his adolescent fantasies. The following morning she woke him by smothering him in compliments and kisses and lovingly prepared a lavish breakfast for him, bringing it to him in the very bed that had been the scene of his exploits, and watching him wolf it down with such a pure and glistening tear in her eye that it almost made her look maternal. Pierre-Emmanuel Colonna's hitherto dreary and tranquil life was swept along on a torrent of sensual pleasure and sometimes, when he gave him his fee, Libero would remark to him with a laugh,

"With the summer I've laid on for you, you ought to be paying me."

At the end of the season they all went out together to a fancy restaurant, with Annie, the waitresses, Pierre-Emmanuel and even Gratas, for what was to be a dinner of thanks and farewell, followed by a well lubricated evening in a nightclub. The following week the girls, apart from Annie, were due to go back to

Mulhouse, Saint-Etienne and Saragossa, but Libero suggested that they should stay. He did not know if he could keep them on all through the winter but the summer season had been extremely lucrative and he could afford to experiment. What he did not admit to them, however, was that his generous proposal derived, in particular, from basely commercial considerations: he was counting on the force of attraction which the presence of four single young women might exert on a region ravaged by cold and sexual deprivation, to fill the bar even in the depths of winter. None of them refused. They were embarked on studies they disliked and knew would lead to nothing, or they had already abandoned them, and no longer dared to make plans, they lived in joyless cities and towns whose ugliness depressed them, and where there was no-one really awaiting their return, they knew that this ugliness would soon start creeping into their own souls and taking hold of them and they were resigned to this, and it was very likely this naive aura of defeat, the magnetic pole of their vulnerability, that had drawn Libero and Matthieu unerringly towards each one of them, Agnès, who sat on the beach rolling and smoking cigarettes, well away from the dancers and the bar, Rym and Sarah, who were sharing a fizzy drink during the voting for a campsite beauty queen, and Izaskun, whom her boyfriend had dropped and dumped there, while they were on holiday, who could hardly speak any French, and who was waiting with her backpack in a dreary nightclub for the day to finally dawn. They did not care about having to share the flat above the bar between five of them, they did not care about the mattresses on the floor and the promiscuity, for they had spent the happiest weeks of their lives at the village, where they had formed a bond they were not yet willing to break, an undeniable bond whose presence Matthieu, too, was aware of during the dinner that evening. For the first time in a long while he thought about Leibniz and took delight in the place he himself now occupied in the best of all possible worlds and he almost felt inclined to bow down before the goodness of God, the Lord of all the worlds, who sets every creature in its appointed place. But God deserved no praise here, for in this little world there was no demiurge other than Matthieu and Libero. The demiurge is not God the creator. He does not even know he is fabricating a world, what he makes, placing stone upon stone, is a man-made work, and soon his creation eludes his grasp and runs away with him and if he does not destroy it, it will destroy him.

Matthieu was delighted to be witnessing for the first time how winter slowly took hold, instead of coming upon it all at once when he got off the plane. Yet winter does not take hold slowly. It does arrive all at once. The sun is still hot in the cloudy summer sky. And then, one after the other, the shutters of the last few houses close, you no longer meet people in the streets of the village. Over two or three days a warm wind blows in from the sea at dusk and then the mist and the cold envelop the last living things. At night the hoarfrost makes the road glitter as if it were strewn with precious stones. That year, for the first time, the winter did not wholly take on the semblance of death. The tourists had gone but the bar did not empty. People came for an apéritif from all over the area, they took part in evening gatherings arranged on Fridays when Pierre-Emmanuel Colonna came back from his week at university, and listened to him singing as he eyed the girls sitting around the fireplace, Gratas busied himself grilling meat and Matthieu had nothing else to do apart from relishing his happiness while drinking spirits that burned in his veins. From time to time, when she had decided it was his turn, he slept with Virginie Susini. She never said anything. She simply came to the bar and settled down at an isolated table where she spent the evening playing patience. When the bar closed and Annie was cashing up she was still there and she stared at Matthieu without a word and followed him when he went home. On each occasion he took her to his room, he tried not to make a noise, so as not to wake up his grandfather. However, sleeping with Virginie was extremely challenging, you had to endure her silence, her fixed, penetrating stare, you had to endure the fact that none of this had any conceivable significance and that nothing justified the feeling he had of having been sullied, but that this was better than going home on his own. For the house frightened Matthieu now, as if at the same time it had been emptied both of the warmth of summer and of any trace of familiar humanity. The portraits of his great-grandparents, which he had always regarded as guardian deities watching over his youth, now took on a menacing aspect and it sometimes seemed to him as if they were not portraits that had been hung on the wall, but corpses, still preserved from decay by the cold, and from which nothing affectionate or tutelary emanated. At night he often heard creaking sounds and hoped they were imaginary, long and mournful, like sighs, as well as the wholly real sounds made by his grandfather wandering about in the darkness, moving from room to room and bumping into the furniture, and Matthieu covered his ears and buried his head under his pillow. If he got up it was even worse. He would switch on the light and find his grandfather in the living room, his brow pressed against the icy windowpane, holding a photograph in his hand that he was not even looking at, or standing there in the kitchen, his eyes focused on something invisible that seemed to fascinatehim and fill him with horror and when Matthieu asked him,

"Alright? Wouldn't you like to go back to bed?"

he would never reply but continued staring straight in front of him, the burden of a millennium of old age overwhelming his fragile shoulders, his jaw trembling, absorbed by this vision that kept him out of harm's way, safe within its terrifying embrace. Matthieu would go back to bed without being able to sleep, and he was sometimes tempted to get into his car but where would he have gone at four o'clock in the morning in the depths of winter? There was nothing for it but to wait until the light of dawn filtered through the shutters to break the curse. The house would then become friendly and gently familiar again. Matthieu would fall asleep. Every day he delayed for as long as possible the moment when he left the bar and he tried at least to go home sufficiently drunk to get to sleep without difficulty. One evening he dared to ask the girls,

"Could I sleep with you tonight? Would you make room for me?"

and he added, lamely,

"I don't want to sleep all alone,"

and the girls burst out laughing, even Izaskun, who had by now made enough progress in French to recognise a foolish remark when she heard one, and they all made fun of Matthieu, and said it was an amazingly original approach and very sweet and they believed him and Matthieu protested his good faith, joining in their laughter, until they said:

"Of course! Of course you can! We'll make room for you."

He followed them up to the flat. There were sleeping bags and piles of bedding neatly laid against the walls. There was incense burning there, too. Annie had her own room, Rym and Sarah slept in the other bedroom and Matthieu went to lie down in the sitting room on the mattress shared by Agnès and Izaskun, which they had hidden behind a Japanese screen. They lay down beside him, still teasing him a little and then snuggled up to him. Izaskun murmured something in Spanish. He kissed them each on the forehead, one after the other, like two sisters, and they went to sleep. No threat now weighed upon Matthieu's slumbers, no deadly shadow. When he awoke his head was resting against Izaskun's breasts and one of his hands lay upon Agnès's hip. He drank a coffee and went to his home to take a shower. But he never slept there anymore. The next night he slept with Rym and Sarah and divided the nights that followed between the mattress in the sitting room and the bedroom, and always slept the same chaste and tranquil sleep, as if the sacred sword of a knight lay there upon the sheet, between his body and the girls' warm bodies, communicating something of its perpetual purity to them. This celestial harmony was only disrupted at the weekend, when Pierre-Emmanuel Colonna joined Annie and they had to endure their satanic frolics. Their staying power was beyond belief. They made a shocking amount of noise, Pierre-Emmanuel puffed and panted and sometimes erupted with incongruous laughter, Annie uttered yells and, to crown it all, she was appallingly loquacious, loudly proclaiming what she would like to do, what was to be done to her, and precisely what was just then being done to her, and the extent to which she had appreciated what had just been done to her, so thoroughly that it felt as if one were listening to the radio broadcast of a sporting event, an obscene and interminable sporting event with a commentary from a hysterical commentator. Matthieu and the girls could not sleep, Rym said:

"He's unbelievable, that guy, I swear he should be timed with a stopwatch,"

and in fact Pierre-Emmanuel began to behave with the arrogance of a sporting celebrity, at the bar he would touch Annie's bottom with assumed nonchalance every time it came within reach, relishing the looks of helpless adoration from the hoi polloi which he imagined to be focused on him, and winking condescendingly at Virgile Ordioni, who laughed nervously, swallowing his saliva, then he would pat Virgile on the back, as if he were a young lad to be gratified with a few fragments of fantasy, which must suffice for him, for that's all he will ever get. It sometimes seemed to Matthieu and the girls that they were listening to a performance whose basic object was to satisfy the expectations of a demanding audience, and then they would begin to applaud and shout "bravo", this caused Pierre-Emmanuel to emerge from the bedroom, sweating and furious, returning to it after looking daggers at them, which then caused them to collapse into fits of giggles, and when the fornicators, overcome with fatigue, allowed silence to reign once more, they went to sleep in their turn, the naked sword blade watching over the purity of their slumbers. But of course the sword was bound to be withdrawn from them eventually and, one night it was. Matthieu was lying on his side, facing Izaskun and once again she murmured something in Spanish and he saw eyes shining in the darkness and a smile that reminded him of Judith Haller, but this was now the world he had chosen for himself, the world he was building, placing stone upon stone, and nothing could make him guilty, he slowly reached out and touched Izaskun's cheek, and she kissed his wrist, then his mouth and she pressed her belly against his and put one leg over his, so that he could come closer and embraced him with all her strength, Matthieu felt overcome with gratitude and beauty, immersed in the limpid depths of baptismal waters, holy waters, waters of everlasting purity, and when it was all over, he rolled onto his back, his eyes open, with Izaskun pressed against him and he saw that Agnès, leaning on her elbow, was looking at them. He turned to her and smiled and she leaned forward and kissed him for a long time, with the tip of her tongue she gathered up a drop of saliva from the corner of his mouth, then, lightly stroked his eyelids with her fingertips, as one piously closes the eyes of a dead person, until he fell asleep beneath her light caress.

"I'm leaving you to look after the bar now, Annie. Have you cashed up?"

Annie gave Matthieu the day's takings and he put them in a little iron box. He opened a drawer and took out an enormous automatic pistol and slipped it into his belt with such a well rehearsed gesture that it now seemed natural.

"Right. Let's go."

Aurélie stared at him in amazement.

"You have a gun now? Are you going completely crazy? What's wrong with you? Have you got issues with your virility? And by the way, you look idiotic. Don't you realise?"

Matthieu did not consider he looked idiotic at all, quite the reverse, but he made no comment on that and simply gave the explanation his sister demanded, faced with which she would have to concur. The bar was doing a roaring trade, it was siphoning off all the clientele from the villages in the area, as far as twenty or thirty miles away, it was incredible, Libero's idea of asking the girls to stay had been a brilliant one for they were the ones who attracted all this custom, without them no-one would be crazy enough to face the rain and black ice simply to come here to a village just like any other and drink pastis that tasted exactly the same as everywhere else, it went without saying, and Vincent Leandri had ventured to point out that thriving businesses run the risk of being held up at gunpoint, especially these days. Of course, human beings had always been thieves since the dawn of time and it's possible to be a thief without being a complete bastard, but these days, and this is the point, people were no longer content just to be thieves, they were complete and utter bastards as well, capable of spending an evening drinking and laughing and kissing you goodbye when they left and coming back ten minutes later in a hood, sticking a gun in your face and nicking your till, then going home to sleep the sleep of the just, and even coming back again next day for the apéritif, just as if nothing had happened, despite the fact that they'd smashed you in the face a couple of times with a rifle butt the night before and smacked Annie twice in the face for good measure, just like that, out of pure villainy, and Vincent was not talking about a potential risk, but something inevitable, there were no ifs and buts about it, sooner or later it was bound to happen, as night follows day, and that was how he'd advised them to buy a gun as soon as possible. Aurélie raised her eyes to heaven.

"So now, if I understand correctly, you not only risk being held up, you may also get killed or kill someone. Brilliant logic.

Well done! You do realise, don't you, that Vincent Leandri is a drunken idiot!"

But she had missed the point, Matthieu had no intention of killing anyone, any more than Libero, the whole thing must be seen as a deterrent, nothing more, and it had indeed taken him some time to grasp all the subtleties of the logic of deterrence, the first time he had to carry the cash box he'd arrived at the bar at about seven in the evening, the pistol slipped inside his trousers, there was a big crowd of people and he'd edged behind the counter where he went through discreet contortions to put the pistol into a drawer without anyone noticing, which was not at all easy, given the number of fellows standing at the counter and the size of the pistol, and Libero had watched his antics for a moment and remarked,

"May I ask what the hell you're doing?"
and Matthieu had replied in a whisper,

"O.K., I'm just stowing the shooter in the drawer,"
and Libero had burst out laughing and Vincent Leandri had burst out laughing as well, and they'd been right to take the piss out of him because when you think about it what's the point of having a gun if no-one knows you've got one? The whole idea, in fact, is for everyone to know you've got one, so that the gunmen, even though they're complete bastards, are going to think it's better to go and do a hold-up somewhere else, where they haven't got a gun, so now in the evening, when he was on duty, Matthieu would

openly remove the pistol from his belt and lay it on the counter for a moment, for everyone to see, and then calmly put it in a drawer, from which he removed it when the bar closed, this was the deterrent, the armed robbers were, let's say, the Cubans, and Libero and he were Kennedy, the method was tried and tested, but Aurélie still sighed and moaned, and would have done so even more if Matthieu had confessed to her that, deterrence or no, the first time he caught a bastard trying to nick his till he was determined to shoot him like a dog.

"And are you going to come back home with a gun?"

Matthieu shrugged.

"Of course not. I'm going to leave it at Libero's place."

He was not keen to have dinner with the family. His parents normally never came for Christmas. This was the first time. And they had insisted that Aurélie should join them too, which the man who was sharing less and less of her life had found very difficult to accept. Since the summer he had only spent a few days with her in October. Instead of going back to France as soon as she was able, she had preferred to accept an invitation from her Algerian colleagues to visit sites at Djemila and Tipasa, claiming that she did not want to offend them. These days she was giving more consideration and attention to people she hardly knew than to him, who had, after all, been sharing her life for several years, yet now he must be content with the small amount of time she granted him with wounding casualness, and, in addition, he had to tolerate her reducing their life together by these extra days she planned to spend at the village with her family, without her even suggesting that he should come with her, as if it went without saying that he wasn't part of her family. And that evening, at table, she was not thinking of him, as she talked about the exceptional richness of a site left abandoned for many years, the trophies, a breastplate swathed in a long bronze mantle, the heads of gorgons that had disappeared from the pediments of marble fountains, the colonnades of the basilicas. She spoke about the kindness of her Algerian colleagues, whose names she was careful not to mis-pronounce, Meziane Karadja, Lydia Dahmani, Souad Bouziane, Massinissa Guermat, about their commitment, about the skill and faith with which, for children from primary schools, they conjured up a city filled with life, and, as the children gazed at this mass of mute stones, the yellow grass became covered in paving and mosaics, the old Numidian king rode by on his great melancholy horse, dreaming of Sophonisba's lost kiss, and centuries later, at the end of the long, pagan night, the faithful, resuscitated, pressed close together against the chancels, as they waited to hear the voice of the bishop who loved them arising within the nave filled with light,

"Hear me, you who are dear to me,"
but Matthieu heard no such voice, he was looking at his watch and thinking about the warmth of Izaskun's arms, as well as those of Agnès, all those things he had no desire to share with anyone,

and when the dessert was placed on the table he declared that he wasn't hungry and was going to leave. But his father said,

"Don't go, please. Stay a little longer, it won't take long,"
and Matthieu remained sitting there, drank a coffee, helped to clear the table and when his grandfather and mother had gone to bed, stood up as well, but his father repeated,

"Don't go, please. I need to talk to you and your sister. Sit down,"
and he began talking to them very calmly and gravely, but without looking them in the eye, he had been feeling tired for some time, he had undergone tests and he was ill, quite seriously ill, and Matthieu heard this perfectly well, but he could not understand why Aurélie's face was crumpling up as his father went on talking and giving them the details of the regime he would be obliged to follow, which would, without any doubt, be effective, a tried and tested regime, almost routine, and yet Aurélie buried her face in her hands and kept repeating,

"Oh, Papa. My God, Papa,"
although he could not be as ill as all that, since he was saying this himself, and Matthieu got up to help himself to whisky, he was vainly trying to concentrate on what his father was saying, but Izaskun's hands were covering his ears, to prevent him hearing and Agnès's hands were brushing his eyelids, as one closes the eyes of a dead person, to prevent him seeing, and despite all his efforts, he could neither see nor hear his father, Jacques Antonetti,

explaining to his children as best he could that he might be going to die soon, because his words had no place in the best of all possible worlds, the happy-go-lucky, triumphal world and within it they could make no sense at all, they were simply a disagreeable noise, the troublesome stirrings of an underground river, whose remote power could present no threat to the order of this perfect world, in which there was only the bar, the imminent New Year, a friend who was like a brother, and sisters whose incestuous embraces exhaled the perfumes of mellow redemption, there was an endless prospect of tranquillity and beauty, which nothing could disturb, so that when Jacques folded him in his arms and kissed him with emotion and said to him,

"Please don't worry, everything will be fine,"
he could only answer in all honesty that he wasn't worried, for he knew everything would be fine and his father replied,

"Yes,"
proud, perhaps, of this son whose great sensitivity had spared him the grievous burden of his distress, and he kissed Aurélie and went to bed. Matthieu remained there at the centre of the living room, as if made vaguely uneasy by some element of uncertainty, he helped himself to another whisky, standing next to Aurélie who was holding back her tears, but he quickly remembered he could leave now and put down his glass. Aurélie looked up at him.

"You do realise?"

"Realise what?"

"Papa may die."

"That's not what I heard. Not at all."

He reached the bar around midnight. Two fellows from Sartène were drinking a bottle of vodka at the counter, they were finding it hard to remain upright but were flirting crudely with Annie, who called them pigs and punished them from time to time with a little reproving caress on their balls, simpering the while and pocketing huge tips. Gratas was pushing a broom around in a corner. All alone at a table Virginie Susini was playing patience. Matthieu went and sat down facing her. She did not pause for a second and did not glance at him. A moment before Matthieu had not felt the need to open his heart to anyone at all but there she was and she might well have been the only person in the world one would not regret sharing confidences with, for it was likely she would not even hear them. He leaned towards her and suddenly said to her,

"Apparently my father may be going to die."

Virginie tossed her head and set down the queen of diamonds beneath the king of clubs before murmuring,

"I know all about death. I was born a widow."

Matthieu made a gesture of irritation. Crazy people wearied him. He wanted to see Izaskun. He regarded Virginie with a smug little pout.

"Well, I don't suppose I'm the one you're waiting for."

Virginie picked up another card.

"No, you're not. He's the one I'm waiting for, but he doesn't know yet,"
and she pointed a finger at Bernard Gratas, at which he stood there, petrified, broom in hand.

And now, watching through the window, she was waiting for the Balearic Islands to appear, offering her the promise of an imminent solace, that of a return to the sweetness of a native land, though not the one she had been born in, and her heart began beating faster until she caught sight of the grey strip of the African coastline and knew she was coming home at last. For it was in France now that she felt in exile, as if the fact of no longer breathing the same air day in day out as her compatriots had made their concerns incomprehensible to her and the remarks they made pointless, a mysterious, invisible frontier had been traced around her body, a transparent glass frontier she had neither the power nor the desire to cross. She had to make taxing efforts to follow the most mundane conversation and, despite such efforts, she still could not manage to do so, she had to keep asking people to repeat what they had just said, or else she gave up responding, and retreated behind the silence of her invisible frontier and the man who would soon no longer be sharing her life at all was constantly upset by this, he would reproach her, but she no longer even defended herself for she had given up the struggle against her own coldness, against the indifference and unfairness that had taken over in her churlish heart. It was only when she reached Algiers airport, and then the university premises, and even more at Annaba, that she became friends again with good nature. She cheerfully endured the interminable wait at the border police controls, the traffic jams and the rubbish tips open to the sky, the water being cut off, the identity checks at road blocks, and, as for the Stalinesque ugliness of the great Hotel d'État in which the whole team at Annaba was quartered, with its dilapidated rooms opening out onto empty corridors, it seemed to her almost engaging. She complained about nothing, her assent was total, for every world is like a man, it constitutes a whole from which it is impossible to pick and choose, and it is as a whole that you must reject or accept it, the leaves with the fruit, the straw with the grain, the vileness with the grace. What lay there, within a casket of dust and filth, were the broad sky of the bay, Augustine's basilica and the jewel of a boundless generosity, whose brilliance outshone the filth and dust. Yet once a fortnight she went back to Paris to spend the weekend with her father. When she had told them he was ill all her colleagues showed her many kindnesses. They gave her quantities of pastries for her father and prayers for his recovery. Massinissa Guermat insisted on going with her to the airport and was waiting for her on her return. At the beginning of April she was sitting with her mother beside the hospital bed in which her father was trying to regain his strength after his treatment. He had shaved his head so as not to see his hair falling out. He asked for a glass of water which Aurélie handed to him. As he was raising it to his lips he dropped it, his eyes rolled upwards and he fainted. Claudie flung herself at him, crying out,

"Jacques,"

and he seemed to recover himself, he looked at his wife and daughter and uttered incoherent words, he grasped Aurélie's wrist and drew her to him, his eyes were those of a dying animal, filled with fear and darkness, and he was trying to speak without managing to do so, despite putting all his energy into it, coming out with a farrago of syllables, sometimes whole words, wrested from the sentences that his sick body cruelly held prisoner, words that were a parody of language and reflected only the desolation of a monstrous silence, much older than the world, and he fell back onto his pillow, his hand still clutching his daughter's wrist. A doctor and some nurses appeared and asked Claudie and Aurélie to leave. They waited in the corridor and the doctor came out to see them, he mentioned kidney failure and uraemia and when they questioned him about what was likely to happen he told them he had no idea and they would have to wait and he left them. Claudie closed her eyes.

"I think you should ring your brother. I can't."

Aurélie went out and when Matthieu picked up the phone she heard laughter and music. At first he seemed unable to understand what she was saying. The treatment was going well, his mother assured him of this every time she rang him, there was no need to worry. She closed her eyes.

"Matthieu, listen to me. He's unrecognisable. He's no longer himself. Can you hear what I'm saying?"

Matthieu said nothing. She could hear the music, voices calling out to one another, more laughter. In the end he muttered,

"I'll go and pack. I'm coming."

The next day, against all expectation, Jacques Antonetti was much better. He had no memory of what had happened the previous day. He tried to joke. He apologised to Aurélie and Claudie for the fright he had given them. The doctor thought it wiser to keep him in hospital. At the hospital they could respond as swiftly as necessary in the event of another incident. If Claudie wished they could install a camp bed for her in her husband's room and she said that would be perfect. Again Aurélie rang Matthieu who was relieved and came close to accusing her of painting an apocalyptic picture when the situation was perfectly under control. She did not trouble to respond.

"So, when are you coming?"

Matthieu pointed out that there was no longer any urgency and he was very busy preparing for the summer season and, besides, if he arrived out of the blue like that there was a risk of alarming his father for nothing, he might well think he'd come to say goodbye, they had to keep up his morale, and Aurélie was unable to control herself any longer, she told him he was a disgustingly selfish little prick, a blind little prick who deep inside him hoped that in the end this blindness would win him absolution, but he would never be absolved for what he was doing now, and if he were to be, it wouldn't be by her, she was not their mother who still saw him as a little cherub who must be shielded at all costs from any painful confrontation with the horrors of existence, as if, deep down, he were the one who deserved all the pity, as if his delicate sensitivity, his exquisite sensitivity, which was apparently his exclusive privilege, excused him from fulfilling his most basic, his most sacred obligations, she was not going to waste her breath speaking of love and compassion to him, these were words he was incapable of understanding, but did he, at least, understand where his obligations lay, did he understand that if he persisted in seeking to avoid them, then he would forever remain the little shit he'd turned himself into in record time, with a skill, she was willing to concede, that took your breath away, and no-one would be able to help him anymore for it would be too late, it would be too late for lamentations or the comfort of regrets, she would be watching out for this, unless he'd become so rotten to the core that he no longer even experienced the reassuring temptation of regrets, but if anything of the brother she loved remained within him, he would force himself to extract his head from his navel and open his eyes, and she wanted to hear no more talk of his being unaware, or unable to see, or too sensitive, however exquisitely and delicately sensitive, there are terrible things in life and you have to face up to them because that's what men do, by confronting them they put their humanity to the test and make themselves worthy of it, and he would come to realise that it was impossible, absolutely impossible for him, totally and conclusively impossible, to let his father die without affording him the charity of a single visit, even if such a visit would be infinitely less pleasant than what made up the daily round of his life as a prick, partying and screwing and the vile stupidity in which he wallowed, like a pig on its dunghill, and when he had realised this he would catch the plane without another minute's delay, and she was so afraid of having to shut him out of her life if she heard the answer he was going to give her now, she was so afraid of having to lose him forever, idiot, incorrigible idiot that she was, that she preferred not to have to listen to his answer and she hung up on him. She went back to Claudie. She was shaking with rage.

"I've just had your son on the phone. You'd have done better to..."

Claudie looked at her, completely lost and defenceless, and Aurélie congratulated herself on not having completed the sentence dictated to her by the brutal impulses of her churlish heart, though she no longer resisted them as soon as she found herself alone with the man who was sharing her life for the last time. She took refuge behind her glass frontier and on that last night she refused to share her body with him, or her anger or her pain. At Annaba Massinissa Guermat asked her how her visit had gone and if her father was getting better, and she replied that everything had gone very well, but as he was taking her back to the vast, silent desert of the Hotel d'État, she surrendered to the wave of sadness overwhelming her and shook her head, no, everything had not gone well, she had thought her father was dying in front of her, he'd been unable to speak, had seized her wrist with all his strength, so as not to be sucked in by the shifting sands that were already filling his mouth and choking him, and there was nothing she could do, because when you die you are alone, oh, how alone you are when you die, and faced with this loneliness she had simply wanted to get away, nothing else, she had wanted her father to let go of her wrist so as to let her get away, and for him to stop compelling her to face this loneliness which is beyond the understanding of the living, and for a long while she no longer felt either compassion or grief but simply a panic fear, the memory of which now filled her with horror and Massinissa said to her,

"I can't leave you like this,"

and she turned to him, with a dry throat, unexpectedly feverish and alive, and said to him in commanding tones, without lowering her eyes,

"Then don't leave me. Don't leave me,"

and without a moment's thought she flung her arms around his neck, and with immense solace felt Massinissa's arms enfolding her. He got up before dawn, so that no member of the team and none of the hotel staff should see him returning to his room. Aurélie waited till dawn. She had a bath and stayed there for a long time in the yellowish water, thinking of nothing, and emerged abruptly to make a call to the man she was going to leave. He was unwilling to believe this, he demanded explanations and, weary of battle, since he needed to have an explanation, Aurélie told him that she had met someone, but this revelation provoked further questions, where? who? since when? and Aurélie replied that none of this had any point because, basically, this encounter had nothing to do with what she was in the process of doing, he must understand this, but he insisted and so finally she said,

"Last night. Since last night."

He went on talking, now there were sobs in his voice, why was she telling him so soon? why hadn't she waited? it could be a passing fancy he would never have known about, she couldn't be certain, and now it was irreparable, why had she confessed something that might well have had no significance, why was she so cruel? Aurélie thought she owed him the truth.

"Because that's what I want: I want it to be irreparable."

Two hours before dawn they were walking with Gavina Pintus on the way to Tenebrae on Holy Thursday night. They had stayed on their feet all night at the bar, so as not to have to wake up, they had cleaned their teeth in the sink behind the counter and were now chewing mint-flavoured gum lest their breath, heavy with drink, might disturb the piety of this night of mourning. For Easter Monday they had planned to arrange a big picnic with music in front of the bar, and the next day they would leave. Libero would travel to Paris with Matthieu, they would go to see his father and combine this with taking several days' holiday in Barcelona, where, without being niggardly over the cost, for they could afford it, they had booked a hotel, thus combining the useful with the agreeable and Jacques Antonetti would not be given the impression that they had come to take their leave of a dying man. So on that night of Holy Thursday they were walking along, arm in arm with Gavina Pintus, keeping as upright as possible, the damp wind froze them, the hold of the alcohol became less noticeable and behind them walked Pierre-Emmanuel Colonna, with the friends from the city of Corte, who had come over to sing in the mass before performing at the party on Easter Monday and they, too, were hastily trying to sober up as best they could. A sleepy congregation packed the church. The electric lights had been switched off. Light came only from the tall candles lit in front of the altar. The smell of incense reminded Matthieu of Izaskun's skin. He crossed himself, stifling a sour hiccup. Pierre-Emmanuel and his friends found themselves a spot in the apse, the text of the Psalms in their hands. They cleared their throats and whispered in one another's ears shifting from one foot to the other. The priest proclaimed that, so that the world might be saved, darkness was about to descend upon the world, as it prepared to put its saviour to death, who was now in tears in the garden of Gethsemane. The singers struck up the first psalm,

In Salem also is His tabernacle and His dwelling in Zion,
their voices filled the church and were marvellously clear. An expression of extreme relief appeared on Pierre-Emmanuel's face, he closed his eyes to concentrate on his own singing and the priest stepped forward and snuffed out one of the candles. You could hear the noise of the rattles and the feet stamping on the wooden prayer stools to bear witness to the end of the world as it sank into darkness,

The earth and all the inhabitants thereof are dissolved,
and now Gavina Pintus looked up towards the cross with the eyes of a frightened little girl, and in the front row Virgile Ordioni was nervously twisting his cap in his hands, as if the whole

village were really going to be swallowed up, there was confusion now between the grinding of the rattles and the noise of shaken foundations, the stones of the church shuddered until the cacophony came to an end and the singing rose up once more,

That the bones which Thou hast broken may rejoice,

and the priest snuffed out the candles one by one. Soon there was only a single flickering flame left, Gavina Pintus took her son's hand as he repressed a sacrilegious yawn, Matthieu was hoping the end of the world would not be as tedious as this, he was cold and sleepy, while over there, in bedclothes so close at hand, Izaskun's body radiated warmth to no avail and the priest raised his tall copper candlesnuffer and it was now completely dark.

The horns of the righteous shall be exalted.

The priest continued speaking in the darkness and said that Christians were not afraid of the darkness from the midst of which he was speaking at that moment, for they knew that it did not mean the triumph of nothingness, the light that had been extinguished was only the light of men and the darkness covered them so that in the end the divine light should appear, for the darkness was its cradle, as the sacrifice of the Lamb proclaimed the resurrection of the Son in the glory of the Father, the everlasting Word, the beginning of all things, and the darkness was not death, for it bore witness not only to the end but also to the luminous beginning, for it was, in truth, one and the same witness. The

144

milky light of dawn crept in beneath the closed doors. After blessing them the priest released his flock, a significant number of whom hurried across to the bar to get over their emotion. Libero made cups of coffee and placed a bottle of whisky on the counter for those whose emotion might really have been too intense. Pierre-Emmanuel was worried about the quality of his performance and Libero assured him that it had been very good, even though, it had to be admitted, polyphonic music was, all in all, boring as hell and hard to take in large doses. Virgile Ordioni who, after drinking his coffee, was reaching out a timid hand towards the whisky, voiced his disagreement.

"It was beautiful! Magnificent! Libero knows nothing about it."

Pierre-Emmanuel patted him on the back with a laugh.

"And what about you? What do you know about it?"
but Virgile was not vexed, he appeared to reflect for a moment, then said,

"That's true. I don't know much about it. But it was beautiful, all the same,"
and there ensued an animated discussion touching on polyphonic music, the various musical abilities of different people, rattles, candles and priests, a discussion crowned by the opportune appearance of another bottle of whisky, and so it was that when Izaskun and Sarah arrived at opening time, they had to turf everyone out into the rain that was just starting to fall. But on Easter Monday the day dawned on a radiant spring. Pierre-Emmanuel

and the men from Corte set up their sound system in the open air and tuned their instruments. Matthieu drank some rosé in the sunlight as he watched Izaskun and raised his glass to her. She responded with a little gesture of her hand, the sketch of a kiss. She was his sister, his loving, incestuous sister. He watched one of the men from Corte whispering sweet nothings in her ear, she laughed, but he was not jealous, he did not care what she might do with this fellow, she was his sister, not his wife, and she would come back to him, no-one could take anything away from him and he enjoyed a formidable feeling of superiority, as if he had been raised up to heights where no-one could harm him anymore. He was amazed that his happiness was unshakeable to this degree and he drank his wine in the warmth of the spring sunshine. The next day he set off with Libero. They gave Bernard Gratas the keys to the bar, they kissed the girls and set off for Ajaccio, waving goodbye and calling out,

"Be good! Don't let the joint go under, whatever you do! See you next week!"

On the road they talked about what they were going to do in Barcelona, they needed to unwind, they certainly deserved it, and they got to Campo dell'Oro airport an hour and a half early. They went into the bar and drank a beer, then another and their conversation slowly petered out. In the end they were completely silent. The passengers for the Paris flight were called to the departure lounge but there was still half an hour to go, there was no hurry and they ordered one last beer. Matthieu looked at the runways and his throat felt dry. His stomach was rumbling unpleasantly. He suddenly realised that for the best part of a year he had never travelled further than ten miles away from the village. Ajaccio was the end of the world. He had never stayed in the same place for so long before. The prospect of flying off to Paris now seemed daunting to him, to say nothing of Barcelona, so remote as to be quite unreal, a place of mists and legends, the earthly equivalent of the planet Mars. Matthieu was perfectly well aware that his fear was grotesque, but he was incapable of struggling against it. He looked at Libero who was staring at his glass with clenched teeth and he perceived that they shared the same fear. They were not gods, but merely demiurges, and it was the world they had created that now held them under the yoke of its tyrannical rule, an insistent voice announced that passengers Libero Pintus and Matthieu Antonetti were urgently awaited before the gates closed, and they knew that the world they had created would not let them depart, they sat there and the final call came, and when the plane had taken off they stood up in silence, picked up their bags and went back to the world they belonged to.

"Where will you go to outside of the world?"

It is a glittering dawn and its brutal light dazzles men's memories and their painful recollections are consigned to the ebb tide of the darkness as it fades, carrying them with it. High up in the dome of Saint Isaac's Cathedral in Leningrad, Christ Pantocrator holds the warhead of an unexploded shell in his long, white hands and it hovers in the air like a dove's feather. One must live and hasten to forget, one must allow the light to soften the outline of all the graves. Everywhere round the abbey at Monte Cassino the long tresses of the North African soldiers spring from the ground like exotic flowers softly caressed by a gentle summer breeze, along the beaches of Latvia the grey waves of the Baltic have polished the bones of children buried in the sand to fashion strange jewels of fossilised amber, over in the sun-drenched scrubland from whence Shulamith will never return to the king vainly calling her, the air is awash with the pollen of her ashen hair, the verdant earth is gorged on shreds of fabric and flesh, it is replete with corpses and rests on nothing other than the vault of their shattered shoulder blades, but this glittering dawn has arisen and in the brilliance of its light the forgotten corpses are now no more than fertile compost for the new world. How could Marcel have clung to the memory of the dead when, after that slow gestation period of war, the world was for the first time opening up the escape routes of its shining pathways for him? All the living were being summoned to the inspiring task of reconstruction and Marcel was among them, dizzy with the infinite number of possibilities, ready to set out on the road, his eyes bruised by the light, wholly focused upon a future that had finally erased death. The new world was recruiting its agents and sending them to take the necessary materials from the colonies for the building up of its hungry and glorious corpus, and from the mines, from the jungles and the high plateaus they were extracting all that its insatiable voracity demanded. Before setting off for French West Africa, where the rivers of the south once flowed, Marcel considered that his new status as a future civil administrator required that he should choose a wife. There were several marriageable girls in the village and Marcel asked his brother, who was at a loose end while waiting to be recalled to Indochina, to make discreet inquiries of their families, to know which of them might look favourably upon a proposal in due course. The next day Jean-Baptiste came to report on the success of his mission and broke it to him that an excess of zeal had unfortunately smashed all his efforts at discretion to smithereens. He had begun his search at the bar by chatting to the elder brother of a young woman from a good family. They had been hitting it off very well to the point of getting drunk together and falling into one another's arms when Jean-Baptiste, acting on impulse, had formally asked him for his sister's hand on behalf of Marcel, who now found himself in a situation all the more delicate because the girl's brother, in his delight, had hurried off at once to his parents, with Jean-Baptiste beside him in a highly emotional state. It was out of the question to risk seriously offending these people by pleading a misunderstanding, the humiliation might have made them resort to violence and Marcel had to accept the young wife jointly bestowed on him by fate and his brother's excessive sociability. She was seventeen and Marcel was consoled by her shy beauty until he realised, after they had exchanged a few words, that she was almost angelically stupid for she was lost in wonder at everything and directed a gaze at her new husband so overcome with admiration that, as the boat taking them to Africa passed beneath the Rock of Gibraltar and sailed out into the waters of the Atlantic, Marcel veered constantly between bliss and irritation. Leaning against the rail, she offered up her innocence to unknown winds and tasted the icy salt from the sea spray with the tip of her tongue, which made her laugh and shiver so violently that she suddenly took refuge in Marcel's arms and he did not know whether he should upbraid her for making such a spectacle of herself or thank her for her childish enthusiasm, he would hesitate for a moment, embarrassed and awkward, but always ended up hugging her to him with all his might, without fear or disgust, for she had the warm and ethereal body of an angel from before the fall, miraculously arisen from a time that still knew nothing of the miasmas of sin and plagues. Through the portholes the distant coastlines were becoming wilder and wilder, great twisted trees leaned out over the waves at the mouths of immense rivers that traced long arabesques of mud across the green waters of the ocean, the heat became stifling and Marcel spent almost all his days in his cabin, in bed with his wife, he let her kneel over his face, bracing herself against the bulkhead with her hands, panting and laughing behind the curtain of her flowing hair, he let her study him and run her hands over him with a schoolgirl's curiosity, frowning, touching every part of his body, as if to reassure herself that he was not a ghost who would soon vanish in the light, he let her settle down in her nakedness, immodestly sitting cross-legged at the end of the bunk and he crawled towards her to lay his head on her thighs and fall asleep for a moment, liberated from the whore in Marseille, for his young wife's caresses had drawn from his veins the last drops of the poison that had infected him and he was no longer afraid of anything. Bodies were no longer reservoirs of pus and blood in the depths of which obscure, malevolent demons lurked and Marcel would have been perfectly happy if he had not been overcome by anxiety every time he had to appear at dinner with his wife, he was perpetually afraid that someone might ask her a simple question to which she would reply so foolishly that the whole table would be struck dumb or else she would not reply at all and open a mouth round with surprise before lowering her eyes and giggling and he was in agony every time she spoke to him in public, he was shamed that she addressed him in Corsican, that ridiculous dialect of whose wretched accent he could never manage to rid himself, and at the same time he was relieved, because nobody could understand what she was saying and he was simply waiting for the moment when he could close the cabin door upon their intimacy which alone put an end to his bitterness and torments. He took on his clerical duties in the offices of the central administration of a big African city which resembled an improbable collection of hovels and mud rather than any city he might have dreamed of, for the world persisted in thwarting his dreams at the very moment when they became real. The smells in the streets were so strong that even ripe fruit and flowers seemed to give off the noxious sweetness of putrefaction, he was constantly repressing feelings of nausea, as he strolled about in the dignity of his linen suit among men and animals over whom there hung the aromas of exotic and savage flesh, borne aloft by the crumpling of brightly coloured fabrics. Proximity to the natives repelled him more every day, he had not come to bring them a civilisation which he himself had known only from a distance and by hearsay in the voices of his masters, but to settle an ancient debt, the repayment of which had been so long deferred, he had come there to live the life that he deserved and which had continually eluded his grasp. He did not rest his hopes in God but in the statutes of the public service, the good news of which had just been promulgated to all the children of the French Republic, which would enable him, without having to pass through colonial service training school, to rise as high as he could in the hierarchy, to extricate himself at last from the limbo he had never entirely succeeded in leaving when he was born. He worked at preparing to take exams as well as at getting rid of the hideous stigmata of his past, his posture, his gait, his accent, in particular, and he forced himself to make his speech flat and clear, as if he had been raised on the estate of a manoir in Touraine, he adopted the affectation of pronouncing his surname with a stress on the last syllable, he worked scrupulously at keeping his vowels open, but to his despair he had to accept that he must continue rolling his "r"s, for when he tried to pronounce an "r" at the back of his throat, all he ever produced was a pitiful choking sound, like the purring of a big cat or the hoarse croaking of a dying man. Jeanne-Marie wrote with the news that André Degorce was due to go to Indochina with a parachute regiment, she told him about her fears and her joy at the birth of a little girl, she gave him a detailed account of their parents' decline and each of her letters was a reminder to him of the unpardonable sin of his origins, even though he now felt equally at ease in offices and at dinners for members of the administration, and attended these on his own, fearing that his wife's presence might break the fragile charm that took him out of himself, while she waited for him at home, safe within the blessed citadel of her innocence, happy and unchanged. She refused to learn anything at all, resolutely speaking Corsican and assisting their African maid with her household tasks, despite admonitions from Marcel, whom she silenced by overwhelming him with kisses and caresses, undressing him standing up, before pulling him over towards the bed where he toppled over with outstretched arms while she closed the mosquito netting around them. He looked at her, he blew gently on her moist breasts, he kissed her on the fold of her groin, her mouth, her nostril, her eyelids, and one day he was surprised by the roundness of the belly on which he lay at rest. She told him she had grown a little fat, her dresses were rather tight. She was eating too much, she knew, and blushing, he asked her when her last period had been, but she had no idea, she had not noticed, and he took her in his arms, took her and lifted her up, the whole of her, with her angelic stupidity, her laughter and the sound of the barbaric language that he no longer wanted to be his own, and allowed himself to be overcome by an absurd joy, an animal joy, of which it mattered little that he did not understand it, for it did not ask to be understood and did not even demand that a meaning should be found in it. She had been pregnant for six months when Marcel, after passing an internal examination, was promoted to be the administrator of an obscure "subdivision" on the outer periphery of a remote "circle", which was not one of hell but simply one featured on the colonial land registry. He now held sway over an immense territory, whose humid lands were populated only by insects, Negroes, wild plants and big cats. The French flag dangled from the end of a pole like a sodden rag on the pediment of his residence, a little apart from a wretched village of huts built on the banks of a muddy river, beside which children used to guide long lines of blind old men at the end of a rope, who trooped along beneath a sky of the same milky white as their dead eyes. His neighbours were a gendarme, whose penchant for drink became a little more manifest with every passing day, a doctor who was already an alcoholic, and a missionary who conducted mass in Latin in front of women with bare breasts and attempted to engage the interest of a resistant audience by repeating the story of the God who had made himself into a man, before dying as a slave for the salvation of all of them. With these men Marcel strove to preserve from extinction the flame of civilisation, of which they were the sole guardians, and dinners were served to them by "boys" dressed as head waiters, who set down gleaming dishes upon impeccably ironed white tablecloths and he allowed his wife, all rotund and smiling, to join them at table because, in the farce he knew he was playing out with his meagre cast of walk-ons, social conventions, blunders and ridicule no longer had any meaning and he no longer wanted to deprive himself, in the name of such things, of the one person who was henceforth the unique source of his joy. Without her the bitterness of his social elevation would have been unbearable to him and he would have preferred a thousand times to be numbered tenth or twentieth in Rome, rather than thus being the governor of a desolate kingdom on the outskirts of the Empire, but no-one would ever offer him such an alternative because Rome no longer existed, it had been destroyed a good long time before and all that now remained were the kingdoms, some more barbarous than others, which it was impossible to escape from, and a man in flight from his own poverty could hope for nothing more than to exercise futile authority over men more impoverished than himself, as Marcel was now doing, with all the pitiless fury of those who have known poverty and can no longer tolerate the nauseating spectacle of it, constantly exacting vengeance for it on the flesh of those who resemble him all too much. It may be that every world is the distorted reflection of all the others, a remote mirror in which excrement appears to shine like diamonds, or it may be that there is only one single world, from which it is impossible to escape, for the escape routes of its illusory pathways all meet together just here, beside the bed in which Marcel's young wife lies dying, a week after giving birth to their son, Jacques. At first she complained of stomach pains and was overcome by a fever that could not be brought down. After several days, having run out of antibiotics, the doctor tried to concentrate the infection in a medically provoked abscess. He folded back the soaking wet sheet, leaned over the sick young woman and pulled her nightdress up from her legs, Marcel leaned over, too, catching the hot aroma of whisky on the doctor's breath as he watched him pricking his wife's thigh with shaking hands, injecting it with turpentine spirit, leaving no more than a tiny red dot on the skin, which Marcel could not take his eyes off for whole days and nights, watching for the moment when all the veins in his wife's body would drain into it the poison that was killing her and he implored her to fight, as if she had the power, through the sole magic of will, to compel her exhausted body to save her, but the white skin of her thigh remained ominously healthy and supple, no abscess ever formed there and Marcel knows she is going to die, he knows it, and, as he kisses her burning brow, he hopes that at least she will never be aware of this, hopes her angelic stupidity will save her to the end, but he is deceived, for stupidity does not save us, not even from despair, and amid her fever she weeps, calls for her baby, caresses and kisses him, and throws her arms about Marcel's neck, saying she doesn't want to leave him, no, no, never, she wants to go on living, then she dozes off for a moment and wakes up in tears, she dreads the darkness, nothing can comfort her and Marcel holds her tightly in his arms without being able to wrest her away from the tide that sweeps her along irresistibly towards the darkness she dreads so much, she is worn out with shivering and tears, and allows herself to be swept away by the tide that eventually tosses her aside, motionless and cold, in a shroud of crumpled sheets. Her face is distorted by terror but it is that of a wax dummy in which Marcel does not recognise the laughing young woman whose innocence and lack of modesty he loved, and for a moment he is overwhelmed by the hope that some element of her, a fragile and delicate breath, like a blithe spirit, might have taken wing from the horror of this stiffened body to find refuge in a place of light, gentleness and peace, but he knows that this is not true, all that remains of her is a corpse whose contours are already collapsing and it is over this relic that Marcel then lets his tears flow. During the funeral he thinks about his family who know nothing yet of his bereavement, he would have liked his mother, well versed in the works of death, to have been at his side rather than the gendarme and the doctor, who sways there under the tropical rain, as the missionary's disillusioned voice reels off one psalm after another over the waterlogged grave. When the stone is laid in place he remains alone for a while and then goes home to rejoin his son, who is suckling with eyes closed from the black breast of the African maid. He detests this baby as he detests this country, regarding them with an implacable hatred because they have conspired together to take his wife from him, when the doctor complains about the lack of antibiotics he refuses to listen to him for he needs scapegoats and has no interest in justice, any more than he is interested in logic, as the sudden fear overtakes him that this detested country might deprive him of the detested child, whom, in turn, he does not want to lose, even though he constantly reproaches him for being born rather than remaining in the limbo no-one wanted him to abandon, and so the slightest gap left between the mosquito net curtains plunges

Marcel into a mortal dread of discovering his son consumed by the monstrous insects that lurk in the stifling depths of the African night, where so many phosphorescent eyes glitter, so many things throng in a seething mass, hungry for Jacques' tender flesh, poised to sink their venomous jaws into it, or deposit their eggs there, and, sensing that he will not know how to protect him, Marcel writes a long letter to Jeanne-Marie. My dear sister, I shall not be able to protect him from the appalling horrors of these climes with their swarms of creatures, I don't want him to die like his mother and I don't want him to grow up without her, please let Jacques find a mother, and gain a sister in your little Claudie, I am well aware of what I am asking you, but, I beg you, who else could I turn to, if not to you, who have never been sparing in your affection, and when Jeanne-Marie, much moved, agrees, he waits until he has leave and can go back to France and hand Jacques over to her. As he returns alone to Africa he weeps, from guilt, maybe from grief, he does not know, but in the depths of his soul he is aware of the huge and murky relief of having managed at one and the same time to save his son and to get rid of him. Once back in his purgatory, he resumed the long, monotonous peregrination of his life, making tours into the bush, passing through villages where dazed children, lined up in order of height, were waiting for him to attribute vague dates of birth to them, so as to revise the administrative records and he dispensed justice with the weary gestures of a fallen god, noting down in minute detail the inept disputes of which the plaintiffs gave him desperate accounts in various languages, including Fulani, Susu-Yalunka, Maninka and all the languages of poverty and barbarism whose accents he now found intolerable, although he forced himself to hear them out in order to hand down judgements whose fairness might restore the saving silence he longed for, and at the time of the cotton harvest he castigated the greed of the Belgian merchants who tampered with their scales, rejecting their proffered bribes with scorn, not because he cared about the interests of the African farmers, but because incorruptibility was the only blue blood he could lay claim to, he kept the records for the collection of the poll tax with inflexible rigour and at nightfall, sitting beside the doctor, he regretted that his ulcer did not allow him to get drunk with him, to escape the terrors of the night. Jeanne-Marie wrote to him that Jacques was growing up and often thought of him, she had had no news of André Degorce after the fall of Dien Bien Phu, but she felt confident, because God would not be cruel enough to rob her of a husband twice. The Empire was slowly falling apart and Jeanne-Marie wrote, the Vietminh have freed André, I'm so happy, Jacques thinks about you and sends you his love, he's growing up so quickly, André will soon be going to Algeria, and Marcel envied his brother-in-law his adventurous life, which contrasted so grievously with the emptiness of his own, he did not perceive how the Empire was falling apart, he did not even hear the muted cracking sounds as its foundations were shaken, for he was entirely focused on the falling apart of his own body, which Africa was slowly infecting with its fertile decay, he gazed at the plants growing on his wife's grave which he would cut down with furious blows of a machete and was convinced that he would soon be joining her, for the demon of his ulcer, sustained by extreme heat and humidity, tormented him more vigorously than ever, as if its demonic intuition enabled it to sense that outside, in the corrupt, clammy air there were countless allies lying in wait to assist it in the final stages of its gradual work of demolition and Marcel kept his eyes wide open at night, hearing the cries of the prey, hearing the bodies of drowsy creatures that had gone astray sliding over the sand as the crocodiles dragged them slowly towards their watery graves, he heard the sharp snap of jaws that threw up showers of mud and blood and, in the turmoil of his own body, he could feel the organs grinding into action, rubbing against one another, to embark on a slow rotation about the orbit of the demon, as, fixed as a black sun, it gave the signal of an upraised hand in the depths of his stomach, and flowers thrust up the tips of their buds in the sockets of his bronchial tubes, the filaments of their roots crept along his veins right to the tips of his fingers, while terrible wars were waged in the barbaric kingdom that his body had become, with their savage victory cries, their massacres of the defeated and a whole tribe of assassins, and Marcel would examine his vomit, his urine, his stools, terrified that he might find gilded clusters of grubs, spiders, crabs or snakes in them, and lived in the expectation of dying alone, transformed into rotting matter even before he died. He kept an intimate journal of his illness, scrupulously noting each symptom, every breathing difficulty, each mysterious rash on his elbow and groin, each bout of diarrhoea and constipation, every worrying discolouration of his penis, every itch and thirst. He thought of his son, whom he would never see again, he thought of his young wife, of her thighs wrapped around his face, and now she seemed so alive that he felt passionate desire for her and then noted down delirium, priapism, necrophilia, morbid preoccupation, before silently approaching the African maid as she dusted the furniture in the dining room, lifting her dress and taking her without saying a word, his arms flapping like the wings of a great vulture hunched over an impassive corpse, and he could only stop when the shame of the orgasm flung him backwards at the last moment, leaning against the wall, his trousers about his ankles, his eyes closed in horror and his penis shaken by ignoble thrustings which the African maid brought to an end by wiping him like a child, with a cloth soaked in warm water, which she then proceeded to use to mop up the puddle of grey seminal fluid on the tiled floor. But he remained alive, for the powers that hounded him were those of life, not of death, a primitive and narrow life, one that begot flowers, parasites and vermin with equal indifference, a life oozing with organic secretions, and thought itself oozed from the human brain as if from a suppurating wound, there was no soul but only fluids governed by the law of a complex, fertile, insane mechanism, the jaundiced concretions of calcified bile, the crimson, gelatinous mass of blood clots in the arteries, sweat, remorse, sobbing and slobber. One night Marcel heard a noise on his veranda, the sound of chairs being overturned, erratic knocking at the door, and when he opened it he found the doctor leaning against the door frame, he was shaking with fever and said, help me, I beg you, I can't see anymore, I'm blind, and when he raised his eyes towards Marcel there were worms gushing out from his eyelids and running down his cheeks like tears. Marcel put him in his own bed for the ten days that the treatment for the filariasis called for, he heard him groaning every time the sheets rubbed against the painful bruises on his legs and his distorted arms, he helped him to endure the appallingly perverse effects of the Notezine, despite the horror inspired in him by this body bloated by a monstrous excess of life which threatened to explode at any moment, with its skin irritations, its lumps, the abscesses that the putrefaction of the vessels beneath the skin had caused to erupt, his eyes red and swollen, like those of a foetus. When the doctor had recovered Marcel was relieved to see him go. He told the African maid to disinfect the house from top to bottom so as to restore the clinical, sterilised universe his burgeoning anxieties called for, he washed his hands in spirit, scrubbed beneath his fingernails until they bled, continued noting symptoms, incipient tumours, septicaemia, necroses, although the only ailment he was suffering from was an appalling loneliness, which he tried to overcome by writing letters daily to his brother-in-law in Algeria, needing to confide in him his certainty of his own imminent death and unbosom himself without restraint, so as to re-establish at least the semblance of a human relationship, even though the one and only confidant he had chosen for himself, and for whom he had a fanatical admiration, never made any reply for, deep down in cellars in Algeria, Capitaine André Degorce, reclusive and mute, was slowly plunging into the abyss of his own loneliness with only his blood-soaked hands for company. Marcel went back to the village to bury his father, then his mother, and did not weep for them because death had always been their vocation and he was almost happy that they had at last been able to respond to a call they must have spent such long years pretending not to hear. He saw his older sisters again and did not recognise them, and also Jean-Baptiste and Jeanne-Marie and his son, whom he no longer dared to embrace and who, in any case, showed no inclination for this. He asked him if he was well and Jacques answered him yes and then he told him he lived far away from him but he loved him and Jacques once more answered yes, and they spoke no more until Marcel's departure for Africa where his promotion to the post of Gouverneur de Cercle awaited him. He took leave of the doctor, the missionary and the gendarme who had been the insubstantial companions of so many pointless years and he left, accompanied by the African maid, and taking with him his wife's remains which he had buried close to his new house. Six months later, without Marcel having noticed anything at all, the Empire ceased to exist. Is this how Empires die, without even a tremor being heard? Nothing has happened, the Empire no longer exists, and as he moves into his office in a Ministry in Paris, Marcel knows this is also true of his own life in which nothing will ever have happened. All the shining pathways have gone dark, one by one, and Lieutenant-colonel André Degorce, after his latest defeat, returns to his wife's arms seeking the redemption he will never be granted as men come heavily down to earth in the new gravitational field of their fallen country. Time has dispensed with hope and continues to pass, unnoticed and empty, to the ever swifter rhythm of funerals that recall Marcel to the village, as if his only constant mission in this world were to see his nearest and dearest into the grave, one after the other, his wife now rests in Corsica, but she died so long ago that he is afraid all he has interred is a few pieces of dead wood covered in clay, and his older sisters die, one after the other, in the precise sequence established by the register of births in its wisdom. In Paris the taste of solitude gradually loses its savour, the cold mists have banished the insects that lay their eggs beneath the skin of translucent eyelids in the white light of the sun, and sealed up the jaws of the crocodiles, the epic struggles are over, he must make do now with pathetic enemies, flu, rheumatism, creeping old age, the draughts in the big apartment in the eighth arrondissement where Jacques has refused to come and live with him, unwilling to give a reason because he cannot admit that he harbours an unspeakable passion for the person he ought to regard as his sister. Jacques is fifteen, Claudie seventeen and Jeanne-Marie weeps hot tears as she relates how she came upon them shockingly naked and in one another's arms in their childhood bedroom, she reproaches herself for her naivety, her culpable blindness, she knew how fond they were of one another, with a love she believed to be tender and fraternal, how much they hated to be separated, but she saw no harm in this, on the contrary, she was foolishly touched by it, while in fact she was nurturing two lewd creatures in her bosom, it is all her fault, she would rather not know how long this horror has been going on and the two of them are not even ashamed of their immorality, Claudie had stood up and confronted her, naked and glistening, fixing her with a defiant gaze that nothing could make her lower, neither reproofs, nor blows, Jacques was sent away to a Catholic boarding school and Claudie now refuses to speak to her parents, saying that she loathes them, and time does nothing to erode her incestuous resolve, a disgraceful secret correspondence is intercepted, for long years Claudie gives them no quarter, she inflicts her tears, her cries, her hysterical silence on them, Jacques runs away from the boarding school to which he is forcibly returned and compelled to undergo a pointless penitence until at length retired Général André Degorce, who is past caring about yet another defeat, once again hoists the flag of surrender and obliges everyone to accept the inevitable disgrace of this marriage, which is finally blessed by the arrival of Aurélie, after the hungry couple have devoted several years to feasting on one another's flesh, for not even the most voracious egotism can escape the immutable cycle of birth and death. Marcel bows his head over Aurélie's cradle, over that of Matthieu, then over the dark, open mouths of the graves that close upon Jean-Baptiste and upon Jeanne-Marie, still in the precise sequence established by the register of births in its wisdom, and then, upon the cold, blood-soaked hands of Général André Degorce, whose heart had already stopped beating long ago. Marcel is alone and when the time comes for him to retire, it confirms what he had probably always known, nothing has happened, those shining escape routes are secretly circular, their course turns in on itself inexorably and takes him back to the detested village of his childhood, and in his suitcase, laid on top of his suits of wool and linen, there is an old photograph, taken during the summer of 1918, in which what had been captured in the silver salts, alongside his mother, brother and sisters, was the enigmatic face of absence. Time is heavy now, almost at a standstill. At night Marcel trundles his old age from room to room in his empty house, in search of the foolish and merry young wife over whose loss he cannot console himself, but all he finds is his father standing there waiting for him in the kitchen. No sound ever escapes his white lips and he peers at his youngest son through the lashes of his burned eyelids, peers at him as if to reproach him for so many missed encounters with worlds that no longer exist and Marcel subsides beneath the weight of this reproach, he knows that no-one can restore his youth, nor does he want this, for there would be no point. Now that he has seen his nearest and dearest into the grave, one after the other, the demanding mission he has accomplished must fall to someone else, and he waits for his perpetually wavering and steadfast health to suffer defeat at last for, in the sequence established by the register of births, his turn has now come to walk alone to the grave.

"For all God has made
for you is a perishable world"

In this village the dead walk to their graves alone – not truly alone but upheld by strangers' hands, which comes to the same thing, and so it is proper to say that Jacques Antonetti took the path to the tomb alone, while his family, gathered together outside the church beneath the June sun, were receiving condolences far removed from him, for grief, indifference and sympathy are manifestations of life, the offensive sight of which must henceforth be concealed from the one who has passed away. Three days earlier Jacques Antonetti had died in a hospital in Paris and the aircraft bringing him home had touched down at Ajaccio that very morning, just when his son Matthieu was getting up from the waitresses' bed and heading down to the bar to make himself a coffee. Libero was already behind the counter dressed in a suit, and starting the coffee machine, Matthieu was grateful to him for being up already to keep him company.

"Did you sleep here?"

Matthieu nodded in confirmation. He would have preferred to be able to spend the past two nights at home, he had intended to do so, and even attempted it the evening before last, but his grandfather had just sat there without saying a word and had not even seemed to be aware of his presence, so that Matthieu, too, had sat there in an armchair staring at the closed shutters and when night began to fall he had got up to light a lamp but his grandfather had said,

"No,"

without stirring, without raising his voice, simply said,

"No,"

and had added,

"That's not the way things are done,"

and made a gesture which Matthieu hastened to interpret as a licence to take his leave, or it may even have been something more absolute and violent, an imperious invitation to distance himself immediately from a solitude that called only for the silence of the night and Matthieu had obeyed, he had freed his grandfather from his importunate presence at the same time as freeing himself and had not been back to see him since. Libero set down a coffee in front of Matthieu and came to sit beside him, scrutinising him from head to toe.

"Are you going to go like that? Are you going to go to your father's funeral like that?"

Matthieu was wearing a clean pair of jeans and a black shirt which he had rather vaguely ironed. He reviewed his attire with a puzzled air.

"Won't this do?"

Libero leaned over and took hold of him by the neck.

"No, it won't. You can't bury your father like that. You smell of sweat. You smell of perfume. You stink. You look dreadful. We'll go to my mother's, and first off you'll take a shower. And then you'll shave. And we'll find you a suit and tie. We'll find something that'll fit you. And it'll all be fine. You'll do everything you have to do. It'll be O.K. You'll see. I promise you."

Matthieu felt the tears welling up into his eyes but they stopped short at the brink of his eyelids, lingering for a moment before retreating abruptly. He caught his breath and briefly hugged Libero before going after him and two hours later as the hearse, followed by an interminable line of cars, entered the village to the sound of the bell tolling, Matthieu was standing there waiting in front of the church, at his grandfather's side, swamped in a suit much too big for him, whose jacket he was under strict instructions not to unbutton for any reason, so that the disgraceful folds in the trousers which a belt now held suspended above his navel should remain hidden. Libero gave him a thumbs-up sign, it's all going fine, and all of a sudden, at the moment when the coffin was being lifted out of the hearse, a crowd of people emerged from their cars and rushed up to him to kiss him in an appalling melee, women who did not know him squeezed him against the black lace of their mourning dresses, his cheeks were sticky with strangers' tears, he caught the pungent smells of eau de cologne, day creams and cheap perfumes, and out of the corner of his eye he could see yet more unknown people jostling one another to hurl themselves at Marcel, and one of the undertaker's men called out,

"Afterwards! Condolences afterwards. After the service!" but no-one was listening to him, and the crowd had backed Matthieu up against the wall of the church and were overwhelming him with their clammy embraces, he felt giddy, he could see his mother holding out her arms towards him and called out to her, but she was trapped by shoals of relentless hands seeking to touch the bruised flesh of bereavement, Aurélie was weeping beside the hearse, overwhelmed by a dense surge of hungry compassion, moist lips proffered well before the contact of the kiss, gold teeth gleaming with saliva between opened lips, and Matthieu felt as if he were dissolving in a soup of human warmth, his shirt was drenched with sweat, the pressure of the belt against his stomach was painful, and then all at once calm descended, the crowd parted to let the dead man through. He was carried by Virgile Ordioni, Vincent Leandri and four of Libero's brothers, and Matthieu followed him, on his mother's arm, for she had finally met up with him, walking beside his grandfather and Aurélie, and, as he entered the church he closed his eyes beneath the soothing caress of the cool air while behind the altar Pierre-Emmanuel Colonna and the men from Corte sang the Requiem. Throughout the ceremony Matthieu searched high and low for his own grief, but could find it nowhere, he gazed at the carved wood of the coffin, at his grandfather's mummified face, he heard his mother's and Aurélie's mingled sobs and nothing happened, in vain did he close his eyes and strive after sad thoughts, his grief did not respond to any of his calls, he sometimes sensed it passing quite close by, his lip trembled slightly from it, and then, at the moment when he thought his tears were finally going to begin to flow, all the sources of moisture in his body ran dry and he abruptly became impassive and desiccated, standing before the altar like a dead tree. The priest swung the censer round the coffin one last time, imploring voices arose within the church,

Deliver me, o Lord, from eternal death,

and the coffin moved off slowly towards the door, Matthieu followed it knowing he was walking behind his father for the last time, but he did not weep, he placed a kiss on the crucifix with a piety he wished was not simulated, but neither his father nor God were waiting for him there in the cross and he felt nothing more than the touch of cold metal against his lips. The doors of the hearse closed. Through her tears Claudie murmured her husband's name, which was also the name of her brother in child-hood, and Jacques Antonetti set out on his walk towards the tomb and he was alone, in accordance with the rule of this village, for the strangers making their way along beside him to the rhythm of his silence counted for nothing. The condolences were interminable. Mechanically Matthieu kept replying,

"Thank you,"

and smiled faintly at the approach of familiar faces. Virginie Susini was radiant and hugged him so tightly that he could feel the slow throbbing of her heart, which had had its fill of death. The waitresses were sitting on a wall, giving time for the crowd to thin out before coming over and Matthieu had to make an effort not to kiss Izaskun on the lips. After half an hour some thirty people were left and they repaired to the Antonetti family home, where Libero's sisters served coffee, eau de vie and cakes. At first conversations were in hushed tones, then gradually louder, a little laughter was heard and soon life returned, pitiless and gay, as always happens, even if the dead are not supposed to know this. Matthieu went out into the garden with a little glass of eau de vie. Virgile Ordioni was pissing against a pile of logs in the corner. Over his shoulder he looked towards Matthieu with his great red eyes. He was full of contrition.

"I didn't want to ask where the toilet was. Because of your mother."

Matthieu absolved him with a wink. He was dreading the inevitable moment when everyone would have left. He dreaded finding himself alone with his nearest and dearest, whose grief he was quite unable to share because his own was still nowhere to be found. At nightfall they would all go to the cemetery together, the stone covering the vault would be sealed, they would be arranging the wreaths and bouquets of flowers, and that is all Matthieu would see, flowers and stone, nothing else, no trace of the father he had lost, not even any trace of his absence. Perhaps he would have been able to weep if he had understood the language of symbols, or if he had at least been able to make an effort of imagination, but he understood nothing and his mind stumbled against the wholly concrete presence of the things that surrounded him, beyond which there was nothing. Matthieu looked at the sea and knew that his insensitivity was no more than an undeniable symptom of his doltishness, he was a creature who enjoyed the constant but narrow happiness animals enjoy, and a hand came to rest on his shoulder, which he took to be that of Izaskun having come into the garden because she was unhappy to see him alone and missed him. He turned and found himself face to face with Aurélie.

"How are you, Matthieu?"

She was studying him without anger but in her presence he lowered his eyes.

"I'm fine, I'm not even sad."

She went up to him and took him in her arms.

"Of course you are. You're sad, you're very sad,"
and the grief he had been hunting for in vain all afternoon was there, wrapped up in his sister's words, far removed from the useless props of symbol or imagination, it swept over Matthieu and he began weeping like a child in Aurélie's arms. She stroked his hair and kissed his brow and made him look at her.

"I know you're sad. But it's no use, don't you see? Your sadness is no use to anyone or anything. It's too late."

On July 15 he received a letter from Judith Haller, telling him that she had passed the exams for her *agrégation* teaching qualification with flying colours, she wanted to share her joy with him, albeit from afar, she expected no reply, she hoped he was happy – was he happy? but Matthieu did not put this question to himself, he stared at the letter as if it had come to him from a remote yet strangely familiar galaxy, one whose glimmering light awoke in him faint echoes of another life. He stowed the letter in his pocket and forgot about it as he began uncorking bottles of champagne in honour of Sarah's departure. She had fallen in love with a horse breeder who had recently asked her to go and live with him, somewhere in the Taravo valley. He was a man of about forty who throughout the winter had been notable only for his suspicious sobriety and his persistence in travelling the miles that lay between the bar and his remote village in the back of beyond whatever the weather. He would settle down at one end of the counter with a sparkling mineral water in front of him, apparently absorbed in mysterious meditation. He did not look at the wait-resses, did not try to touch their buttocks or make them laugh, even going so far as to politely refuse Annie's caresses of welcome, and it was impossible to guess at what moment and by what means he had somehow managed to form a romantic attachment to Sarah, who now had her arms around his neck and was covering him with kisses and making him drink champagne. Pierre-Emmanuel was singing love songs with comic emphasis, he put down his guitar to be given a drink and ruffled Virgile Ordioni's sparse hair as he pointed to the happy couple,

"Just look at them, Virgile. One day you might find yourself a sweetheart too!"

and Virgile blushed and laughed and said,

"I might, why not? You never know,"

and Pierre-Emmanuel tweaked his ear and shouted out,

"Oh, you dirty old man! So you fancy the girls, do you? You're a right one, you are!"

and picked up his guitar again, not sparing the tremolos, and embarked on the tale of a young woman so beautiful that her godmother could only have been a fairy. At two o'clock in the morning Sarah got her things together, loaded them into her new partner's mud-spattered 4x4 and came to say her farewells. Rym cried as she hugged her and made her promise to send news of her happiness, Sarah promised to do so and wept a few tears as she kissed each of the people she was leaving, she told Matthieu and Libero that having met them was the best thing that had ever happened to her, she would never forget them, the place she was going to would be always their home from home, which the horse breeder from Taravo confirmed with a nod, and Matthieu watched her leaving with an almost paternal emotion, for he was convinced that his protective shadow would forever extend over Sarah's life. Matthieu was particularly pleased with himself and was vexed to note that Libero did not share this happy mood, he was pacing up and down impatiently, going out onto the terrace for repeated consultations with Vincent Leandri, and berated the girls for persisting in their foolish sobbing instead of finishing their work and clearing the floor before going off to snivel in bed, or wherever, if that was what took their fancy. When the girls had left Annie suggested remaining behind to receive any insomniac customers who chanced by. Libero looked daggers at her.

"No! you push off as well. You'd do better to get some sleep. You look an absolute wreck."

She opened her mouth to say something but changed her mind and went out without a word, leaving Libero alone with Vincent Leandri and Matthieu, who seemed at a complete loss.

"Is it seeing Sarah go that's made you lose it like that?"

"No. It's Annie. She's robbing us, the bitch. I'm sure of it."

Since the start of the season Annie had adopted the habit of staying behind in the bar after closing time, which an arbitrary by-law had unreasonably fixed at three o'clock in the morning. When Libero or Matthieu had gone home with the contents of the till and the revolver in his belt, she remained heroically perched on her stool behind the counter, ready to serve the last of the drunkards who were scouring the area in search of a hospitable haven where they could complete their excursion into alcoholic oblivion. In the unlikely event of a visit from the forces of law and order she could claim that the bar was closed, the till cashed up and she was simply enjoying a private drink with friends. She only made up the receipts at the very last moment, when it was certain there were no kepis at large in the area. At first this stratagem, which could only be applauded as an act of civil resistance to the tyranny of the State, made everyone happy: the wandering drunkards, overwhelmed with gratitude, could now count on a stopping-off place, Annie was rewarded for her devotion by generous tips, which were added to her overtime payment, and the bar's turnover was increased. It could sometimes happen, of course, that Annie waited for customers in vain, and indeed this was occurring more and more frequently, but this did not alert Libero until Vincent Leandri chanced to mention to him that some friends from Ajaccio had dropped in for a drink the previous Saturday after leaving a club, although Annie had told him she had not seen anyone that night. Libero asked Vincent Leandri if he was certain of the date and what drinks his friends had had and in what quantities, so Vincent had rung and asked them to confirm for themselves that his information was correct. Libero was incensed and it seemed nothing would calm him, in tones of fatalism tinged with wisdom Vincent pointed out that waitresses had always helped themselves from the till, it was a law of nature and vainly urged him to be indulgent, while Matthieu kept repeating that it was not as serious as all that, but he refused to listen to them, he wanted to unmask Annie by catching her in the act, it was the only way to do it otherwise she would completely deny everything, the bloody whore, the tart, the vile bitch, and he only calmed down when he had found a way to arrange the *in flagrante delicto* that his vengeful fury demanded. He recruited a group of young people in the town, making sure that Annie did not know any of them, and gave them money they were under orders to spend in the bar down to the last centime the following night. They were to claim they were just passing through the area and had no plans ever to set foot there again, and, above all, they must keep a careful note of all the drinks they had had, prior to making a precise report to Libero of what they had consumed, a mission they carried out to the letter. So the next day, when Annie came on duty in the afternoon, Libero was waiting for her in the bar with a big smile.

"You had a few people in last night."

His smile froze for a moment when Annie replied "yes" and handed over the money together with the till receipts. Libero counted it and his smile returned.

"Not many people, then."

No, not many, just a couple of fellows from Zonza who'd stopped off for a drink for a few minutes on their way home, she'd

186

waited there and closed up at about five in the morning, it had been a long night, it couldn't work every time, but no matter, and then Libero started to yell, paying no attention to the customers who nearly jumped out of their skins,

"When are you going to stop giving me all this crap?"
and he yelled that he knew Annie had had more customers but Annie replied,

"No! That's not true! It's not true!"
pouting stubbornly like a little girl, and he went up to her with clenched fists, describing each of the young people and reeling off a list of what they had drunk and telling her what they had paid, piling on the evidence relentlessly until all she could do was to burst into tears and beg for pardon. Libero said nothing. Matthieu thought, with relief, that the episode was finished, that Annie would get away with a proper dressing-down and the threat of punishment the next time she put a foot wrong, she would pay back the money and everything would begin again as it had been before, she said it herself,

"I was out of order. I'll pay it all back. I'll never do it again, I swear it."

But Libero's silence was not one of forgiveness and he had no intention of letting Annie repay her debt.

"I don't want you to pay it back. Keep what you've taken. I want you to go up to the flat, right now, and pack your bag and get out. I don't ever want to see you again. You're out. Now."

Annie pleaded with him, she swore through her tears never to do it again, one after the other the customers got up and left the bar so as not to witness any more of the scene and Annie pleaded again, she'd been out of order but she'd also done good work, he couldn't do this to her, where would she go? he didn't realise, she was forty-three, he didn't realise, he couldn't kick her out like that, like a dog, and she repeated her age again, she was on her knees now, she reached out her hands to Libero who remained unmoving, eyeing her with a look of hatred, forty-three, he didn't realise, she'd do everything he wanted, everything, and the more she wept the more Libero grew rigid beneath his protective shell of hatred, as if this woman before him on the ground were the incarnation in her quaking flesh of an absolute evil of which the world must be purged at all costs.

"I shall come back in an hour's time, and, in an hour's time, you won't be here."

When he had gone she got up unsteadily and Rym took her arm to help her climb up to the flat. Matthieu did not dare look at her, a painful burden weighed on his chest, but he understood neither its nature nor its origin, he was waiting for night to fall and life to resume, without any further surprises, for he had once more become a little child who only finds reassurance in the perpetual repetition of what is the same, far away from ill-formed concepts whose unpleasant stirrings came to trouble his mind before bursting like bubbles on the surface of a swamp, he was waiting for the taste of the alcohol, for the constant tension that kept him sharp, his nerves on edge, alert for no purpose, and he was waiting for the moment of going to bed, Izaskun's skin and Agnès's eyes, despite the weariness, despite the acrid heaviness of breaths laden with champagne, gin and tobacco, the thick saliva that clung to stained teeth, sleep would come later, despite heavy eyelids, despite the strangeness of this impetus towards a body as exhausted as his own, which gave off the same toxins in damp sheets, and nothing would close his eyes in dreamless sleep before the unfolding of the nocturnal rite ordered by the law of this world, which was not the law of desire, for desire counted for nothing, any more than the weariness or the vulgarity of orgasm, and for each of them what mattered was to play their part in this choreography that validated their waking up in the morning, and kept them on their feet so late into the night. Thus are all worlds based upon ludicrous centres of gravity from which they secretly derive all their equilibrium and, as Rym took up her station behind the counter in Annie's place, Matthieu rejoiced that the stability of this equilibrium had not, in the end, been threatened, he did not sense the subtle tremors in the earth, across which a network of fissures was opening up, as intricate as a spider's web, he did not notice the timid reticence with which the girls now approached Libero, even though he was once more relaxed and smiling, everything was happening for the best, Pierre-Emmanuel did not appear to be alarmed at Annie's disappearance, he had learned a Basque song to please Izaskun, and Matthieu did not notice the black looks he was darting at Libero over the top of his microphone, Izaskun confessed that she didn't know a word of Basque, she'd grown up in Saragossa, she smiled, everything was happening for the best, Matthieu drank and noticed nothing, but how could he have noticed anything at all, he who had still not succeeded in believing that his father was dead? At two o'clock, Pierre-Emmanuel folded up his microphone stand, rolled up the cables and put away his guitar. Libero gave him his fee.

"You could have told me about Annie, don't you think?"

Libero tensed as if from an electric shock.

"Mind your own fucking business, you arsehole! O.K.? Mind your own fucking business."

Pierre-Emmanuel stood there dumbfounded for a moment, put the money in his pocket and went to pick up his guitar.

"That's the last time you'll speak to me like that."

"I'll speak to you any way I like."

Pierre-Emmanuel left, head bowed, and the bar remained frozen in silence. Matthieu again felt that mysterious burden sliding down from his chest to his stomach and asked Libero what the matter was. Libero gave him a big smile and filled up their glasses.

"That's how it is with those arseholes. If you're nice to them they screw you. They're too stupid. Niceness. Weakness. They don't know the difference. It's too hard for them. You have to use the language they understand. They understand that very well, believe me."

Matthieu nodded and went to sit outside with his drink. He gazed sadly at the darkness, reflecting for the first time that perhaps his eyes did not see the same things as those of his childhood friend. He took Judith's letter from his pocket, re-read it and, paying no attention to the time, took out his mobile.

After an interminable wait of three hours which had done nothing to appease her anger, Aurélie was seen by a member of the consular staff. The dig was finished, they had not found Augustine's cathedral but there was so much still to do, one day they would find it and once again the marble of the apse where the bishop of Hippo had lain dying, surrounded by praying clerics, would gleam in the sunlight. Aurélie had invited Massinissa Guermat to come and spend a couple of weeks with her at the village and he had just told her he had been refused a visa. Outside the embassy walls covered in barbed wire stretched a queue three hundred yards long in which men and women of all ages were stoically waiting their turn to be told that the sets of papers they had in their hands were not acceptable, for want of some item they had never been asked for. Aurélie went straight to the security door and asserted her status as a Frenchwoman to gain access but the receptionist had made her pay for the privilege by asking her to go and sit in an armchair where she had taken good care to forget all about her. The staff member was wearing a striped, short-sleeved shirt and a hideous tie and within a few minutes it became clear to Aurélie that she was not going to be given the explanation she had come for, no-one was going to agree to re-examine Massinissa's file, for their only concern here was to take a loathsome delight in wielding a power manifested only through arbitrary capriciousness, the power of the weak and pathetic, of whom this individual in his short-sleeved shirt was the perfect representative, with the smug, idiotic smile he directed at her from the impregnable citadel of his own stupidity. At the next desk an old woman in a hijab was clutching a little girl to her, and wilting beneath a deluge of contemptuous reproaches, her papers were a total shambles, they were filthy and illegible, good only for the rubbish bin, while Aurélie stubbornly pursued her fruitless strug-gle, employing the inoffensive weapon of reason, Massinissa was a doctor of archaeology, he held a post at Algiers University, did they think his situation was so unsatisfactory as to make him dream of abandoning it for the honour of working illegally on a building site in France? She herself was a university lecturer, did they think she spent her spare time setting up clandestine immigration networks? It was simply a matter of a few days of holiday, after which Massinissa would return to Algeria in a proper manner, this she would vouch for, but the individual in the short-sleeved shirt remained impassive and she longed to jab him in the arm with the pair of scissors that lay on the leather blotter on his desk. She left the consulate in a state of unspeakable rage, she wanted to write to the consul, to the ambassador, to the president, to say that she was ashamed to be French and the attitude of the staff she had had dealings with was a disgrace both to them and to the country they were supposed to represent, but she knew it would serve no purpose and she resolved to go to the village on her own, for a week, at least, before meeting up with Massinissa in Algiers in August. She needed to see her mother and, even more, her grandfather. She could not abandon him. However distressed she was by her father's death, she was certain that Marcel was still more distressed by it, beyond what she herself could imagine, for it was in the normal order of things for children to bury their parents, but the appalling disruption of this order added outrage to grief, she wanted to go back to her evening walks with him, taking his arm, and she did so scrupulously, touched to feel him leaning on her, so fragile and so very old. After he had gone to bed, for want of other possible distractions, she went to have a drink at the bar. The young guitar player had made some progress, his vocal technique had improved but he still had a deplorable penchant for schmaltzy ballads, preferably Italian, which he sang with his eyes closed, as if to hold in check the massive surge of his emotion, before receiving the plaudits with the modest air of one who is confident that they are richly deserved. He strolled nonchalantly over to the counter, fully conscious of the female eyes upon him, and made open fun of Virgile Ordioni who laughed in his disarmed innocence, and Aurélie sometimes wanted to slap him as hard as she could, as if the poisonous atmosphere that now prevailed in the bar had contaminated her, too. For the atmosphere really had become poisonous, the scent of a storm hovered in the air, standing at the counter the men coarsely eyed up the tourists' deep cleavages and sunburned thighs, unconcerned about the presence of husbands who were forced to accept endless rounds of drinks, not bought for them out of kindness but with the palpable intent of making them legless, Libero was constantly being obliged to intervene almost physically, with all the weight of his young authority, and Matthieu looked completely out of his depth. Aurélie almost felt sorry for her brother, he really seemed like a child and basically he was a child, exasperating and vulnerable, one who could only protect himself from the threat of nightmares by taking refuge in an unreal world of childish dreams, a world of sugar candy and invincible heroes. The day before she left Aurélie met Judith Haller, whom Matthieu had invited for the holidays and whom he favoured with the sight of himself slipping the pistol into his belt when the bar closed, clearly interpreting the young woman's look of consternation as an admiring and silent homage to his manliness. Happily inhabiting his role as the *patron* of a bar, he offered drinks to Aurélie and Judith, for whom more distress was in store, since it would be given to her that very evening to witness a spectacle particularly rich in decibels and gushing tear ducts. Judith was sipping her drink and chatting with Aurélie when a howl, like that of a wounded animal, made her jump. Out on the terrace, her head buried in her hands, Virginie Susini was rocking backwards and forwards yelling and sobbing and allowing no-one to come near her. Apparently, in an incomprehensible recovery of his dignity, Bernard Gratas had just for the first time refused to be summoned to mate with her, and had furthermore grandly insisted that in future he was not to be treated like a breeding boar and Virginie, who had at first remained impassive, had abruptly launched into a fit of hysterics worthy of the great hall at the Salpêtrière mental hospital from which nothing was lacking, no twitch, no muscular spasm, there was even an attentive and delighted audience, she moaned that she wanted to die, that she was already a lifeless corpse and called out Gratas's Christian name, she howled that she needed him, news of the greatest significance, albeit highly unexpected, which gave the scene all its dramatic interest. Oh, she needed him, she desired him, why was he rejecting her? she was filthy, she was ugly, she wanted to die and when Gratas, surprised but moved, went up to her and touched her hand, she flung her arms about his neck and kissed him full on the mouth while still weeping, and he returned her kiss with such ardour that Libero had to ask them sharply to go and fornicate somewhere other than in front of his bar. The remaining customers exchanged coarse comments, Virginie was a madwoman and Gratas, it was now as clear as daylight, was a wimp of a Gaul, and everybody laughed, but Judith was not laughing. Aurélie tried to reassure her.

"I don't think it's like this every night."

The next day Aurélie kissed her mother and grandfather goodbye, promising to come back and see him soon, she was sad to leave him, but she wanted to get some fresh air and to see Massinissa. She urged her brother to take good care of their grandfather and pay some attention to Judith, whom she abandoned to her uncertain fate, wishing her a good holiday.

He could no longer remember why he had telephoned her in the middle of the night to invite her to stay with him. Perhaps he had wanted to prove to himself that he was sufficiently remote from the world she represented for him no longer to have to fear it or run away from it, there were no longer two worlds, but just one now, a world that remained unified in its sovereign magnificence and it was the only world Matthieu belonged to. He was no longer afraid of Judith carrying him off with her or reviving within him the painful after-effects of his former duality, he wanted to show himself to her as he was now, as he had always dreamed of himself being, but she could not see it. She spoke to him as if he had not changed, picking up the threads of old conversations whose sense was now lost on him, and it was like conversing with a ghost. She described in detail how her *agrégation* oral exams had gone, the sound of the little bell in the Descartes lecture theatre, the familiar Sorbonne building immediately transformed into a sacrificial temple with its officiating priests and its victims, its cruelty, its martyrs and its unlikely miracles, she dreaded the German exam, she had prayed for a question on Schopenhauer and had almost fainted on reading the name of Frege on the paper she had drawn at random but grace had descended upon her, everything swiftly seemed to fall into place, as if the god of logic himself had been leaning over her shoulder, and Matthieu nodded automatically, even though he did not want to hear anything about Frege, or Schopenhauer or the Sorbonne, he was thinking about Izaskun, with whom he could no longer sleep because he had had to return to the family home during Judith's visit, so as not to abandon her to the gloomy company of his mother and grandfather, although he was dying to do so, and he looked forward impatiently to the blessed moment when he would take her to the plane. Indeed, she did not seem very happy at the village, she was forever suggesting ridiculous plans for cultural excursions, she wanted to go to the beach, she said Virgile Ordioni frightened her and the drink gave her bad headaches. Matthieu tolerated these obvious manifestations of bad faith insofar as this enabled him to make Judith responsible for his own unhappiness. One night, apparently one like any other, Pierre-Emmanuel remained sitting in a corner of the main bar area for no obvious reason while the girls were cleaning the room, and when they had finished, Izaskun turned to him and they left together. A slow trickle of lava made its way into Matthieu's entrails. He kept his eyes fixed on the door as if he hoped to see them returning and Judith put her hand on his arm.

"Are you in love with that girl?"

It was a stupid question, clumsy in its formulation, to which he could not offer an answer for it seemed to him that love and jealousy had nothing to do with the unbearable pain now consuming him. Izaskun was his sister, he reminded himself, his tender, incestuous sister, at the bar he never showed her any signs of affection, he had no need to mark his territory in public, as most men like to do, and no-one observing them would have thought that there was anything whatever between them, and what was there between them, if not this intimacy of shared sleep and the performance of the rite that guaranteed the stability of the world? In the name of what should he have felt jealous? And he reminded himself: what could be taken from him that would not in the end come back to him? But it had become impossible for him to feel superior and invincible, the foundations of the world had been shaken, the cracks were becoming chasms and the next day Izaskun spent the whole evening throwing moist glances Pierre-Emmanuel's way, she broke off serving to go and kiss him and cling to him, despite remonstrations from Libero to which she responded by muttering obscene Iberian curses, and Matthieu simply had to admit to himself that he was well and truly dying of love and jealousy, even though he did not recognise his beloved sister in the amorous, purring pussycat now flaunting her fatuous passion night after night, and he knew perfectly well she would never come back to him, he could not prevent himself from thinking about Pierre-Emmanuel's sexual exploits, he saw precise, intolerable images, he heard the cries that Izaskun had never uttered with him and he transferred all his hatred onto Judith, whose arrival had set the signal for the apocalypse. She was a foreign body which the world was rejecting with abrupt eruptions of chaotic violence. Plenitude and harmony were at an end. Disaster followed disaster. Judith and Matthieu were waiting for Libero to finish cashing up before going for a drink in a nightclub when Rym rushed into the bar in T-shirt and pants, looking completely panic-stricken, all her money had disappeared, a year's worth of tips and savings which she used to keep in a little box hidden under her clothes, that nobody knew about apart from Sarah and now she couldn't find it, she could no longer remember exactly when she'd last seen it, she talked about plans she could never bring to fruition, her young woman's dreams, dreams no-one had ever bothered to find out she might be cherishing, she wanted help, she wanted to search the flat from top to bottom, without accusing anyone, although there must be a guilty party, of course, and she refused to listen to Libero who said it would probably be pointless, they must search, and search now, and they turned the flat upside down, going through stuff belonging to Agnès and Izaskun, who took this questioning of their honesty particularly badly, they lifted up boxes of drink in the storeroom and under the counter, without finding anything and Rym kept shouting that they must go on looking. Libero tried to reason with her but she would not listen to him and in the end he lost his temper.

"For fuck's sake! There are banks, aren't there? You must be a halfwit to keep your cash here! It's gone. You'll never see it again. Get it? It could be anyone at all, one of those thieving bastards who come to rob us, it might even be me, if you like. But it makes no difference in any case, because you'll never see that cash again. You'll never see it."

Rym bowed her head and fell silent. There was no longer any question of going down to a club. On the way home Judith stopped without warning and burst into tears.

"What's the matter? Is it Rym?"

Judith shook her head.

"No. It's you. I'm sorry. It really upsets me to see you like this."

Matthieu took her sympathy as an insult, the worst, in fact, that had ever been addressed to him. He tried to remain calm.

"Look, I'll take you to the airport. Tomorrow."

Judith dried her tears.

"Do."

He was certain he would never see her again. He did not know that he would soon understand how much those wounding words overflowed with love, for nobody had loved him, nor ever would love him, like Judith, and several weeks later, in the night of pillage and blood that would reduce the world to ashes, it was of Judith that he would think and it would be to her that he would turn, again regardless of the time, immediately after ringing Aurélie. The world was not suffering from the presence of foreign bodies but from its own inner decay, the sickness of ancient empires, and so Judith's departure solved nothing. After a few days Rym handed in her notice and no-one thought of keeping her on. She had become sullen and bitter, since the night of the search she had been on very bad terms with Agnès and Izaskun and she could no longer bear the thought of possibly rubbing shoulders with the person who had robbed her of her future. Gratas was charged with replacing her at the till but it was not easy for him to concentrate on his work with Virginie constantly coming to toy with him, so they now had to reckon with the presence of two couples on heat whose combined efforts disturbed the smooth running of the business. Libero wore himself out with a whole range of reactions, from entreaties to threats, but in vain. Pierre-Emmanuel delighted in infuriating him, he would give orders to Izaskun who obeyed them with servile haste, as if he were the boss, he would summon her to the microphone and thrust the full length of his tongue into her mouth, as well as giving her buttocks an energetic massage, and Libero was on the brink of a nervous breakdown.

"That little bastard! I'll end up smashing his head in."

Pierre-Emmanuel had perfected his little game developed in the days of Annie, which took the form of provoking the frustration of the luckless by presenting them with the spectacle of his own sexual fulfilment. Virgile Ordioni was his favourite victim. He showered him with intimate confidences, he asked him with mock ingenuousness what he would like to do with a woman if he could manage to find himself alone with one, offering for Virgile's consideration a spectrum of practices, each more salacious than the last, from among which he was supposed to indicate what his preference was, Virgile laughed, choking on his own saliva, he went purple and Libero again tried to intervene.

"Why don't you leave him alone?"
and Pierre-Emmanuel protested his good faith and friendship, patting Virgile on the shoulder, who hastened to support him.

"Oh, let him be! He's a good lad, he is."

Pierre-Emmanuel was not a good lad, Libero knew very well, but he did not want to be so cruel as to open Virgile's eyes to his tormentor's true nature and went back to the counter, hissing between his teeth,

"Little bastard,"
bearing the bitter cross of his resentment until closing time. He would go down to the town with Matthieu, who delayed for as long as he could the moment of going back to his childhood bedroom, the exile to which Izaskun's inconstancy had condemned him, they would do the rounds of the clubs, sometimes sleeping with tourists on the beach or in car parks, and went back to the village at dawn, drunk as lords, their foreheads pressed against the windscreen of their car, as it zigzagged along the edge of the precipice. Towards the end of August Vincent Leandri invited them out to a restaurant and they left Gratas in charge of the bar. The

town was beginning to empty of its tourists, a pleasant breeze was blowing over the harbour, life seemed sweet and they were enjoying the relief of spending a whole evening well away from the bar. They were not worrying about what might be going on there and if Gratas and Pierre-Emmanuel were to decide to hold an orgy on the billiard table, they could screw themselves silly as far as they were concerned and good luck to them. They ate lobster and drank white wine and Vincent suggested they go for a drink at the bar owned by the friend who had introduced them to Annie. To get away from the village only to end up in a tart's bar did not seem like a tremendously appropriate idea but they wanted to oblige Vincent. The friend once again welcomed them with open arms and immediately treated them to a bottle of champagne. In one corner of the room bathed in scarlet light the girls were chatting as they waited for customers. A great fat oaf came in and settled at the other end of the counter, where a girl came and joined him. Snatches of their conversation reached Matthieu, the fat oaf was trying to impress, uttering idiotic remarks and coming out with appalling jokes to which the girl responded with laughter so forced that it sounded almost insulting and Matthieu recognised Rym's voice. It was her indeed, in a black dress and high-heeled shoes, her face disfigured by make-up. Matthieu pointed her out to Libero and they were about to get up from their stools to go and greet her when she stopped them in their tracks by focusing a fixed stare on them before slowly turning away and starting to laugh again as if nothing had happened. They did not stir. The champagne was growing warm in their glasses. The fat oaf ordered a bottle and went to get comfortable in a private alcove. Rym prepared a tray, an ice bucket and two glasses, and went to join him there. She gave Matthieu and Libero one last look before drawing shut a pair of thick red curtains.

"Let's go."

In the car Vincent tried to be reassuring, that's how life was, there was not much to be done about it and still less to be said, girls like that didn't generally make it to Buckingham Palace, very rarely, in fact, and though one could deplore it, that's how it was, nobody was to blame. Life. Libero's jaw was clenched.

"They're all going to end up like that. All of them."

He turned to Matthieu.

"We did that."

Matthieu was afraid he was right. The demiurge is not God. That is why there is no-one to absolve him for the sins of the world.

That time was gone: he could no longer go to her in the night, walking softly along the empty corridors at the Hotel d'État; she no longer waited for him to come with a pounding heart. The moments they now spent together were heavy with the weight of of other people's stares. From time to time they went to spend the day at Tipasa, to get away from Algiers. They stopped for a meal at Bou-Haroun, the purplish fish innards on the stones of the quayside were boiling in the sun and the slightest breeze drove a miasma of decay towards the restaurant terraces, but they went on eating and refilled their glasses with red wine served in Coca-Cola bottles. In the afternoon they would walk about the site together, occasionally stepping on a used contraceptive left behind by a couple who, like them, had no bedroom as a haven for their embraces, but they did not seek to emulate these al fresco raptures, for something that might have passed for a blissful act of transgression by lovers became here nothing more than the mark of sordid necessity. The month of August had just ended, a month of scorching heat, fish innards and humidity, a month without love. Aurélie understood that there was only one place where she could live out her relationship with Massinissa in freedom and that place was neither France nor Algeria, it was located in time, not space, and did not lie within the limits of this world. It was a part of the fifth century that lived on in the collapsed stones of Hippo, where Augustine's shade still celebrated the secret weddings of those who were dear to him and could not achieve union anywhere else. Aurélie was sad, she had never been one whose passions were swiftly aroused, sentimentality appalled her, but she would dearly have loved to know where this affair might lead her. She was ready to accept all setbacks, provided they were to herself and she found it particularly painful to have to give in to the harsh reality of facts that corresponded to no-one's intention. For she had no other choice but to give in. Once more the frontier of a transparent glass wall arose around her which she still had not the power either to pass through or to break down, although this might now be her dearest wish. Massinissa would take her out to eat kebabs with him in the Draria district, they would sit down in the family room of a working-class restaurant, where the service was much too fast and efficient and the meal did not last more than a quarter of an hour, which they tried to prolong by drinking their mint tea as slowly as possible, and Massinissa would pay, and they would drive around in Algiers, at the road blocks the police checked their papers, looked them up and down with a mocking air and he drove her back to the hotel where he could not follow her. She wanted to give him a treat and invited him to the Chinese restaurant at the Hotel El Djazaïr. It was an appalling evening. Aurélie decided not to send back the third bottle of corked Médéa. Massinissa, petrified at first, was now darting furious looks at the waiter as he set down their chicken spring rolls in front of them, wearing a most unpleasant, enigmatic grin, Massinissa was convinced he was mocking him, and only addressing him as "Monsieur" with such emphasis to make him feel that, despite the presence of the Frenchwoman, he was a mere peasant. He was getting angrier and angrier,

"You don't know these bastards and their contempt. That flunkey, he's so damned pleased with himself,"

he did not touch the food on his plate and in the end Aurélie called for the bill, which she paid with her credit card. The waiter presented her with the voucher for her to sign, while grinning at Massinissa who grabbed hold of his waistcoat discreetly and said something to him in Arabic. The waiter's grin vanished. They went back to their car. Massinissa went on brooding bitterly.

"I couldn't afford to take you to a restaurant like that. Entrées costing five hundred dinars. And those are not places for me, in any case."

Aurélie understood him. She squeezed up against him in the car. She managed to persuade him to let her pay for a room for him in the same hotel as herself, so that they could spend a night together, they would pretend not to know one another, he would come to her room silently, as at Annaba, but she could clearly see that he felt deeply ashamed of his situation as a kept man and felt this shame affecting his desire at the very moment when he took her in his arms. After two days Massinissa returned to his parents' home. That was how it was. The dig was finished, they had slowly returned to their respective worlds and they were reaching out to one another across an abyss that nothing could bridge. It is an illusion to believe that one can choose one's native land. Aurélie had no links with this country, apart from the blood her grand-father, André Degorce, had caused to flow there and the elusive remains of an old bishop, dead many centuries before. She brought the date of her departure forward and packed her bags without saying anything to Massinissa. What could she have said to him? How do you walk away from a person with whom you have no quarrel, whom you wish you did not have to walk away from? What could they have done other than exchange foolish remarks? And she was afraid that if she saw him again her desire to remain with him might persuade her to postpone her departure pointlessly. She did not leave him a letter. She did not want to leave him anything other than her absence, because it was by her absence that she would always haunt Massinissa, just as a kiss from a vanished princess forever haunted the Numidian king who bore his name. She telephoned her mother to say she would be in Paris that evening. At the airport she did not allow herself the least gloom as she went through the departure routines. She looked at the Balearic Islands through the window and when she saw the coast of Provence she dried her reddened eyes. Claudie had prepared a meal for her.

"Are you alright, Aurélie? You look tired."

She replied that everything was fine, kissed her mother and went to sleep in her childhood room. At four o'clock in the morning the ringing of her mobile phone brought her out of a dream in which a strange wind was blowing across her body and slowly burying her beneath the sand and she knew she ought to seek shelter but did not want to withdraw from the warm caress of this wind, a caress so gentle that she was still thinking about it as she picked up the telephone. She heard gasps, sobs, choking and then Matthieu's voice.

"Aurélie! Aurélie!"

He kept saying her name over and over again and could not stop weeping.

There were no barbarian hordes. Not a single Vandal or Visi-goth horseman. It was just that Libero no longer wanted to run the bar. He would wait till the end of the summer season or until mid-autumn, he would find work for the girls, a proper job, and then he would help his brother, Sauveur, and Virgile Ordioni on the farm, or he would go back to his studies, he didn't know, but he no longer wanted to run the bar. He didn't like what it had become. Matthieu felt as if he had been betrayed. What was he to do? Libero shrugged his shoulders.

"Can you see yourself spending a lifetime here? The procession of girls trooping through, always the same stupid girls. The little bastards like Colonna. The drunks. The hangovers. It's a crap job. A job that turns you into an idiot. You can't live off human idiocy. I thought you could, but you can't because you end up even more idiotic than the rest. Honestly, Matthieu, can you see yourself staying here? in five years' time? Ten years?"

But Matthieu could see himself staying there perfectly well. In fact he was utterly incapable of imagining a different future. It was true the summer season had been difficult, but they were over the worst now. They couldn't just walk away like that, after all, it was good what they'd done for the village, everything had been so dead before, they'd brought life back to it, people came now, they were happy, they couldn't chuck it all in just because of one rather difficult season.

"The people you're talking about are suckers who come here and spend all their cash to get laid by girls they're never going to get laid by anyway, and who are too stupid to go straight to the whores. Sometimes I think I prefer things here when it's dead. And anyway I'm tired. And I want to be able to look myself in the eye in the mirror."

What was all this rubbish about not being able to look himself in the eye in a mirror? Was the wretched state of things in the world their fault? They were neither crooks nor pimps and, even if they closed the bar, lots of girls would still be going on the game. If Rym had finally found her vocation as a whore what could they do about it? Wasn't this a tendency they all had anyway, like Izaskun?

"Don't talk shit, Matthieu. Not you."

It was the last Saturday evening in August. Pierre-Emmanuel's friends from Corte had come to take part in a big late night concert. They set up the sound system on the terrace, the customers took their seats and Virgile Ordioni unloaded the charcuterie from his van. At half past midnight the musicians put down their instruments and left the stage to applause. They positioned themselves at the counter beside Virgile, who was drinking eau de vie in

213

a corner while waiting for Libero to have a little time to come and keep him company. Pierre-Emmanuel patted Virgile on the shoulder.

"Well, well, what a pleasure to see you! Bernard, a drink for me, and a drink for my friend Virgile!"

Libero was out on the terrace chatting with a family of Italians. From time to time he glanced inside the bar. When Izaskun passed close by Pierre-Emmanuel he caught her by the waist and kissed her on the neck. She gave a shrill little cry. Libero went inside.

"Izaskun, get on with your work, damn it. Bernard, you go and deal with the sandwiches on the terrace. I'm taking over from you."

Libero sat down on the stool behind the till and leaned over towards Pierre-Emmanuel.

"I've told you a hundred times. Let her get on with her work and wait till closing time before you get your end away. That's not too difficult to understand, is it?"

Pierre-Emmanuel put his hands up in a gesture of surrender.

"Ah! It's so hard when you're in love! Have you ever been in love, Virgile? Tell us about it."

And now all the men from Corte insisted on hearing about Virgile Ordioni's love life, he laughed and said there wasn't much to tell, but they refused to believe him, it wasn't true, they were sure Virgile was a great ladykiller, go on, tell, Virgile, no need to be shy, he was among friends, how did he snare his women? Did he sweet talk them? On the dance floor maybe? Oh yes! Poetry! He wrote poetry for them, that was it, wasn't it? Come on, they wanted to know, they'd be happy with one conquest, just one, for instance, why didn't he tell them about the very latest woman to succumb to his charms, just one conquest, that wasn't too much to ask, was it? he could tell his friends everything, but perhaps he was shy, he needed a more congenial setting for spilling the beans, all he had to do was to come down to a club with them, and then he could tell them all over a good bottle, no? He would tell them all, wouldn't he? how he'd seduced her, what he'd done to her in bed, whether she'd yelled out, but the only snag was that they wouldn't let him into a club looking like that, not with his great mountain boots, at any rate, no way, and in his work clothes too, that wouldn't do at all, there were rules, it was no joke, and then, in any case, all things considered, it'd be a mistake to take a ladykiller like Virgile into a club, he'd help himself to all the available women in no time at all and there wouldn't be a single one left for anyone else! After all, you have to leave some for the others! It was only fair. You mustn't be selfish, you've got to think about people who've come a long way, all the way from Corte, it wasn't very good manners not to give them a chance, they'd never come there again, no, so after all it wouldn't be a very good idea to take him to a club, and Virgile was still laughing and saying he'd be glad to tell them, if only he had something to tell. Libero heaved a sigh.

"I suppose you think that's funny. Why can't you leave him in peace?"

"Oh! Fuck off! We're having a good laugh! we're very fond of him, our Virgile."

Oh yes, they were very fond of him, but he was giving them a poor return for their affection, he was being secretive, he could at least tell them about his fiancée, he must surely have a fiancée, up there in the mountains, to keep him warm in winter, a big, fat, greasy shepherdess, for example, who smelled of goat, he must have one of those in reserve, Virgile, no? unless he doesn't like fat women, quite apart from the problem of body hair, ah well, if you're a bit choosy, and she's a fat shepherdess who smells of goat and doesn't wax her pussy, there's nothing to be done, but maybe you'd rather have her hanging round your neck all the same, you don't want to screw just anything that comes along, that's very understandable, that's how it is when you're fussy, you prefer fresh young girls, with everything shaved, their thighs, calves, pussy, everything, yes, that's much better, and Pierre-Emmanuel embarked on the praises of Izaskun, a truly fantastic, well-shaved pussy, smooth as your hand, like a baby's skin, and so warm, quite out of this world, especially at the fold of her thigh, where the skin is so soft, did Virgile see what he meant, such soft skin, so you could feel the warmth of it when you touched it with your lips? and Virgile laughed nervously and began looking down and became hunched up in his corner, Libero

216

banged his fist on the counter, but Pierre-Emmanuel went on, leaning over Virgile and speaking into his ear, it was out of this world how soft Izaskun was, and it was especially out of this world when she took your dick in her mouth, you wanted to shout out, could Virgile imagine that? could he imagine? and one of the fellows from Corte gave a cry of ecstasy and another of them burst out laughing and said,

"How do you expect him to imagine it? Goats don't suck you off, you know!" and they all began laughing while Virgile subsided on his stool with the remnants of his own laughter trapped in his throat like a groan. It was almost two o'clock. The bar had emptied. The girls were sponging the tables. Libero bellowed:

"That's enough."

His eyes were standing out on stalks. Pierre-Emmanuel did not at once get the measure of what was happening. He grasped Virgile by the shoulder, the latter did not stir.

"Are you his mother, or something? Virgile doesn't need you, you know! He's perfectly . . ."

"You stupid little bastard!"

Matthieu drew closer. He saw Libero's right hand half opening the drawer beneath the till.

"You're a stupid little bastard, and you're going to fuck off out of here right now along with your stupid fucking friends . . ."

"Hey! Watch your language!"

". . . I said, with your stupid fucking friends, that's you, you and you, in case I've not made myself clear, those three little bastards there, you're going to fuck off out of here, and as for you, take a good look at this bar, take a good look now, because once you've left it, and as long as I'm here, you'll never set foot in here again, and if you ever do think of coming through that door, do you understand, as soon as you set your foot in here, I'll smash your face in, and if you think I'm joking, just try it now, go out and try coming back in again, you little fucker! just try it!"

Pierre Emmanuel and his friends stood there for a moment facing Libero, who now had his hand in the drawer.

"O.K., let's go."

Pierre-Emmanuel put his arms round Izaskun and gave her a lingering kiss, just beside Virgile.

"I'll see you at the flat in a minute."

As he was walking to the door Matthieu saw that his hands were shaking slightly. At the door, however, Pierre-Emmanuel turned and looked back at Libero.

"I know what's in that drawer. I'd keep your hand on it, if I were you. O.K.?"

"If you come back without your friends, I won't need it. Don't you worry about me."

Libero placed both hands on the counter and took a deep breath.

"Right. Let's clear up and close."

Izaskun came back into the bar carrying a tray laden with dirty glasses which she set down on the bar. Virgile stared at her open-mouthed, his eyes blank. She met his gaze and started shouting at him in Spanish. Libero told her to go to bed, he came round the counter and took Virgile by the arm.

"Here, come along. Come with me."

He made him sit out on the terrace in the fresh air and brought him a bottle of eau de vie. Virgile did not stir. Libero crouched down beside him and talked to him for a long time, he spoke in the language Matthieu would never understand, for it was not his own, he spoke in a voice filled with tenderness and warmth, clasping his hand, and it was a warmth that had no beginning and no end. From time to time Virgile shifted his head. Libero left him alone on the terrace. He told Gratas he could go home to be with Virginie and poured out two glasses. He gave one to Matthieu.

"I don't know if it was such a good idea to humiliate him like that."

"What else could I do? I don't give a fuck about that idiot. If he wants a fight, I'll give him a fight and that'll be that. I'll give it to him even if he doesn't want it."

The night when the world came to an end was tranquil. Not one Vandal horseman. Not one Visigoth warrior. Not one virgin with her throat cut amid burning houses. Libero cashed up, with the pistol laid on the counter. Perhaps he was thinking nostalgically about his student years, about those texts he had sought to make a bonfire of on the altar of the world's stupidity, echoes of which nevertheless still came back to him.

For all God has made for you is a perishable world, and you yourself are destined to die.

A car stopped outside the bar. Pierre-Emmanuel got out. He was alone. He paused on the terrace and looked at Libero through the open door. But he did not try to come in. He passed close to Virgile Ordioni, ruffled his hair and remarked in genial tones,

"It's time to go in and give her one,"
and he walked towards the waitresses' flat. Libero looked down at the till. Outside there were dull thuds, and a squeal more strident than the screaming of the rattles at the Tenebrae service. Libero came running out of the bar, pistol in hand, followed by Matthieu. The street lighting was switched off but by the light of the moon, right in the middle of the road, they could see the vast, shadowy figure of Virgile Ordioni crouched over Pierre-Emmanuel who was squealing and squealing. Virgile was seated on his chest, clamping his arms beside his body, while his legs beat frenziedly against the tarmac, he had lost one shoe and was giving desperate heaves with his hips to break free, while Virgile snorted violently through his nose, like an enraged bull, pulling Pierre-Emmanuel's trousers down along his thighs before ripping the thin fabric of his underpants, Matthieu was unable to move, he watched the spectacle frozen to the spot, and Libero threw himself at Virgile's shoulders, trying to tip him over, shouting out,

"Virgile! Stop! Stop!"

but Virgile did not tip over and did not stop, and it was as if he were giving himself a heavy shake, swinging an arm round behind him, and Libero fell flat on the road, his face turned up towards the stars, and Virgile dealt blows with his big clenched fists at Pierre-Emmanuel's legs and pinned his knees to the ground with one hand, while with the other he opened the knife he had taken from his pocket, Libero began shouting,

"Stop! Stop!"

but the incessant whirling of the knife kept him at bay, he went behind Virgile just as Pierre-Emmanuel began squealing louder than ever, at the cold touch of the blade against his lower abdomen and Libero was now hammering on Virgile's shoulders and the back of his neck with the butt of the pistol, but the latter remained unshakeable and contented himself with making sweeping gestures, as if he were chasing away a fly, before starting to rummage with his fingers between Pierre-Emmanuel's legs, where he was bringing in the knife once more, prior to breaking off, for Libero was getting in his way, and knocking him to the ground once more with a back thrust of his arm, and Libero got to his knees, hearing Pierre-Emmanuel uttering a squeal that no longer had anything human about it which froze his blood, threw an imploring glance at the still unmoving Matthieu and began shouting once more,

"Virgile! I beg you! I beg you!"

but his shouting was in vain, the squealing rent the night and Libero stood up in one movement, cocking the pistol and holding out his arm, straight in front of him. He fired at Virgile Ordioni's head and Virgile crumpled on his side. Pierre-Emmanuel crawled away as if he were escaping from a fire and remained sitting there, his trousers lowered, shaking in all his limbs and groaning without being able to stop. He had grazed legs and a bloody gash on his pubis. Libero went up to Virgile and fell to his knees. There were brains and blood on the tarmac and the corpse was still shudder- ing with convulsions that soon came to an end. Libero covered his eyes and repressed a sob. He got up for a moment to look at Pierre-Emmanuel's wound and went back to sit beside Virgile, taking his hand and raising it to his lips. Pierre-Emmanuel was still groaning and, from time to time Libero would say to him quietly,

"Shut your mouth. There's nothing wrong with you. Shut up," and he put his hands over his eyes and sobbed, before saying again,

"Shut your mouth,"
and waving his pistol vaguely at Pierre-Emmanuel, who was repeating,

"Shit, shit, shit, shit,"
without being able to stop, and Matthieu stared at them, unmov- ing in the moonlight. Once again the world had been overcome by darkness and nothing would remain of it, no trace. Once more

the voice of blood rose up towards God from the earth below in the rejoicing of broken bones, for no man is his brother's keeper, and soon it became still enough for the melancholy hooting of the owl to be heard in the summer night.

The sermon on the fall of Rome

Aurélie sits beside the bed where her grandfather lies at rest. He can let himself go without fear into his obscure dreams of a dying man as she is keeping watch for death's approach on his behalf and her sentinel's eyes are not dimmed by weariness. The doctors have granted Marcel Antonetti the remarkable privilege of dying at home. They could fight against his illness but not against the demon of extreme old age, the ineluctable falling apart of an already ruined body. Blood rushes to his stomach. The heart gives way before the assault of its own beating. At each intake of breath the pure air sets the dried-out flesh on fire and it is slowly being consumed like resinous crystals of myrrh. Twice a day a nurse comes to change the drip and assess the rate of his decline. Virginie Susini brings meals from the bar that Bernard Gratas has prepared for Aurélie. Since yesterday Marcel has completely given up eating. Claudie and Matthieu have caught the plane and will be arriving during the course of the day. Aurélie would have preferred them not to come but Matthieu insisted. Judith would remain alone in Paris with the children for as long as was necessary. In eight years he has only returned to

Corsica once, to give evidence at Libero's trial, at the court in Ajaccio, but has never set foot in the village. He has not changed. He still believes looking the other way suffices to dispatch whole sections of his own life into nothingness. He still believes that what one does not see ceases to exist. If Aurélie had listened to her churlish heart she would have told him to stay put. It was all too late now. There was no need for him to bother coming here to act out the masquerade of redemption. But she said nothing and now she waits. In the bedroom the shutters are half closed. She does not want the excessively bright light to hurt her grandfather's eyes. But nor does she want him to die in darkness. From time to time he opens his eyes and turns his head towards her. She takes his hand.

"My dear girl. My dear girl."

He is not afraid. He knows she is there keeping watch on his behalf for death's tranquil coming, and he sinks back into his pillow. Aurélie does not let go of his hand. Death may arrive sooner than Matthieu and Claudie, thus favouring this intimate communion of theirs, and, when it comes, along with Marcel, it will carry away the world that now lives on only in him. All that will remain of this world will be a photograph, taken in the summer of 1918, but Marcel will no longer be there to look at it. No child in a sailor suit now, no little girl of four, no mysterious absence, only a pattern of lifeless marks, with no-one left to make sense of them. The truth is that we do not know what worlds are.

But we can watch out for the signs of their coming to an end. The release of a shutter in summer sunlight, a tired young woman's delicate hand resting on that of her grandfather, or the square sail of a ship sailing into the harbour at Hippo, bringing with it, from Italy, the inconceivable news that Rome has fallen.

For three days Alaric's Visigoths had pillaged the city and trailed their long blue cloaks in the blood of virgins. When Augustine learns of this he barely pays attention to it. He has been battling for years against the fury of the Donatist heretics and is dedicating all his efforts, now that they are overcome, to bringing them back into the bosom of the Catholic Church. To those of the faithful who are still animated by the spirit of vengeance, he preaches the virtues of forgiveness. He is not interested in the collapse of masonry. For although he has cast out far away from himself, with horror, the heresies of his own culpable youth, he may yet have retained from the teachings of Manichaeus the profound inner conviction that this world is bad and does not merit the shedding of tears over its ending. Yes, the world is filled with the darkness of evil, he still believes this, but he now knows that no spirit animates this darkness, for that would challenge the unity of the eternal God, since darkness is only the absence of light, just as evil is simply the trace left when God withdraws from the world, an infinite distance separating the two, which only His grace can bridge in the pure waters of baptism. If men's hearts will open to the light of God, let the world pass into darkness. But refugees are daily bringing the poison of their despair into Africa. The pagans accuse God of failing to protect a city even though it had turned Christian. From his monastery in Bethlehem Jerome immodestly broadcasts his lamentations throughout Christendom, unreservedly bemoaning the fate of Rome, now overcome by fire and the assaults of the barbarians, and in his blasphemous sorrow he forgets that Christians do not belong to the world, but to the eternity of the things eternal. In the churches at Hippo the faithful share their distresses and doubts and turn to their bishop to learn from his lips what black sin it is that has brought such a terrible punishment upon them. The shepherd must not reproach his flock for their fruitless fears. He must simply allay them. And it is for this purpose that in December 410 Augustine comes to his flock in the cathedral nave and takes his place in the pulpit. An immense crowd has come to listen to him, squeezed up against the chancels, waiting in the soft light of winter for the voice to arise that will release them from their pain.

Hear me, you who are dear to me,

We Christians believe in the eternity of the things eternal to which we ourselves belong. God has promised us only death and resurrection. The foundations of our cities are not embedded in the earth but in the heart of the Apostle upon whom the Lord chose to build his Church, for God does not raise citadels of stone, flesh and marble for us, outside of this world He raises the citadel of the Holy Spirit for us, a citadel of love that will never collapse and will forever stand in its glory when the things of this world have been reduced to ashes. Rome has been captured and your hearts are outraged by this. But I ask you, you who are dear to me, is not despairing of God, who has promised you the salvation of His grace, is that not the true outrage? Do you weep because Rome has succumbed to the fire? Did God ever promise that the world would live for ever? The walls of Carthage fell, the fire of Baal was extinguished, and Massinissa's warriors who brought low Cirta's ramparts have vanished in their turn, like sands before the wind. You knew that, yet you believed Rome would not fall. Was not Rome built by men like yourself? Since when do you believe men have the power to build things that are eternal? Man builds upon sand. If you seek to cling fast to what man has built you are clinging only to the wind. Your hands are left empty and your heart isafflicted. And if you love the world you will perish with it.

You are dear to me.

You are my brothers and sisters and I am sad to see you thus afflicted. But I am yet more sad to find you deaf to the word of God. What is born in the flesh dies in the flesh. Worlds perish, passing from darkness into darkness, one after the other, and however glorious Rome may be, it still belongs to the world and it must perish with the world. But your soul, filled with the light of God, will not perish. The darkness will not swallow it. Do not shed tears over the darkness of the world. Do not shed tears over palaces and theatres destroyed. That is not worthy of your faith. Do not shed tears over the brothers and sisters whom Alaric's sword has taken from us. How can you bring God to account for their deaths, He who gave His only son in sacrifice for the remission of our sins? God spares whom He wishes. And those whom He has chosen to leave to die as martyrs rejoice today that they have not been spared in the flesh, for they live forever in the eternal blessedness of His light. It is this and this alone which is promised, to us, who are Christians.

You who are dear to me,

Do not grieve either over these attacks by the pagans. So many cities that were not Christian have fallen and their idols could not save them. But as for you, is it a stone idol that you worship? Remember who is your God. Remember what He has foretold unto you. He has foretold that the world will be destroyed by fire and the sword, He has promised you destruction and death. How can you be made fearful by the fulfilment of these prophecies? And He has also promised that His son will return in glory amid these fields of destruction, so that the eternal reign of light may be established, in which you will take part. Why do you weep instead of rejoicing, you who live only in anticipation of the end of the world, at least if you are a Christian? But perhaps it is neither seemly to weep, nor to rejoice. Rome has fallen. It has been captured, but the earth and the heavens have not been shaken by this. Look about you, you who are dear to me. Rome has fallen but is it not, in truth, as if nothing had happened? The stars are not troubled in their courses, night gives way to day, which is followed by night, at every moment the present arrives from nothingness and returns to nothingness, you are here, before me and the world is still travelling towards its end but it has not yet reached it and we do not know when it will reach it, for God does not reveal everything to us. But what He reveals suffices to fill our hearts and helps us to find strength in the test, for our faith in His love is such that it saves us from the torments that must be endured by those who have not known this love. And it is thus that we keep a pure heart, in the joy of Christ.

Augustine pauses for a moment in his sermon. In the crowd he sees expectant faces, many of which have now become serene. But he still hears some stifled sobs. Very close to him, against the chancel, a young woman looks up at him, her eyes veiled in tears. At first he looks at her with the severe expression of an angry father, but he sees she is smiling strangely at him through her tears, he makes a sign of benediction over her and twenty years later it is this smile that comes to his mind, as he lies there on the floor of the apse while kneeling clerics pray for the salvation of his soul, of which no-one is in any doubt.

Augustine lies there dying in his own city to which for three months Genseric's forces have been laying siege. Perhaps all that had occurred in Rome in August 410 was the shaking of one centre of gravity, the setting in motion of a slight swing of a pendulum, the thrust of which finally propelled the Vandals through Spain and across the sea, all the way to beneath the walls of Hippo. Augustine's strength has ebbed away. He has been so weakened by privation, that he can no longer stand. He can no longer hear either the clamour of the Vandal army or the frightened voices of the faithful seeking refuge in the nave. To his exhausted mind the cathedral now seems once more to have become a haven of light and silence protected by the hand of God. Soon the Vandals will be unleashed upon Hippo. They will bring in their horses, their brutality and the Aryan heresy. It may be that they will destroy all that he once loved, with his sinner's weakness, but he has preached about the end of the world so often that he must not now be concerned by it. Men will die, women will be defiled, the Barbarian cloak will once more be dyed in their blood. The ground upon which Augustine rests is everywhere marked with the Alpha and Omega, Christ's sign, which he touches with his fingertips. God's promise is constantly being fulfilled and the soul of a dying man is weak, vulnerable to temptation. What promise can God make to men, He who knows them so little that He remained deaf to the despair of His own son and did not understand them, even when He made Himself one of them? And how may men have faith in His promises when Christ himself despaired of his own divinity? Augustine shivers on the cold marble and just before his eyes are opened to the eternal light that shines on the city no army will ever capture, he wonders in anguish whether all those in tears among the faithful whom the sermon on the fall of Rome failed to comfort had not understood his words better than he understood them himself. Worlds perish, in truth, passing one after the other, from darkness into darkness, and perhaps the succession of them signifies nothing. This unbearable thought burns Augustine's soul and he heaves a sigh, as he lies there amid his brothers, and tries to turn towards the Lord, but again he sees that strange smile, bathed in tears, that the candour of an unknown young woman had once bestowed on him, bearing witness, before him, to the end and at the same time to the beginning, for it is one and the same witness.

JÉRÔME FERRARI was born in Paris in 1968. He worked as a professor of philosophy in Algiers for four years before moving to Corsica and then to Abu Dhabi. He came to international prominence in 2012 when he won the Prix Goncourt for *The Sermon on the Fall of Rome*.

GEOFFREY STRACHAN is the renowned translator of Andreï Makine. His translation of Makine's *Le Testament Français* was awarded the Scott-Moncrieff Prize.